MANGA MATH MYSTERIES

#5

THE ANCIENT FORMULA

A Mystery with Fractions

by Melinda Thielbar

illustrated by Tintin Pantoja

D1057639

GRAPHIC UNIVERSE™ · MINNEAPOLIS · NEW YORK

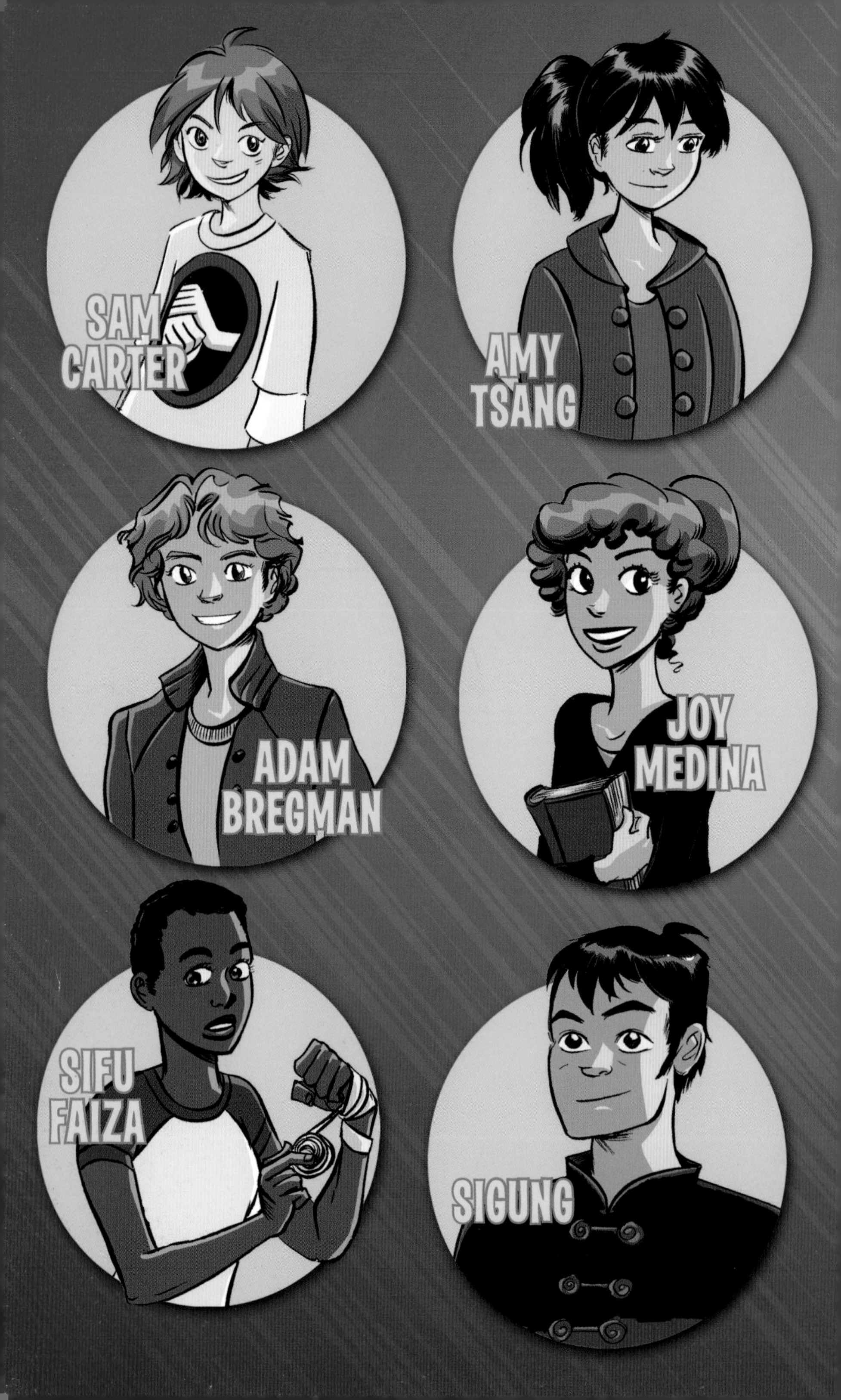
SAM CARTER
AMY TSANG
ADAM BREGMAN
JOY MEDINA
SIFU FAIZA
SIGUNG

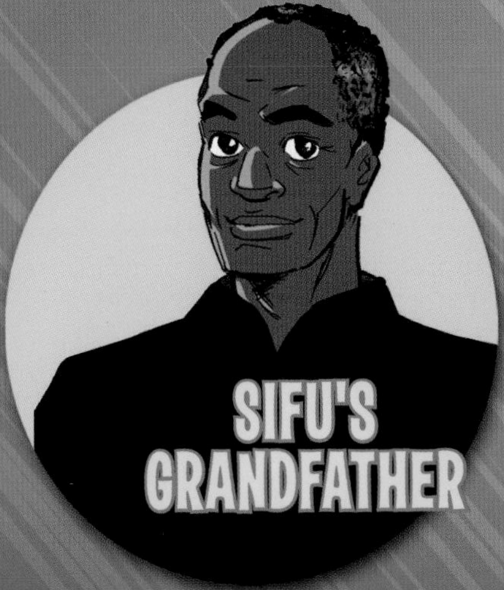
SIFU'S GRANDFATHER

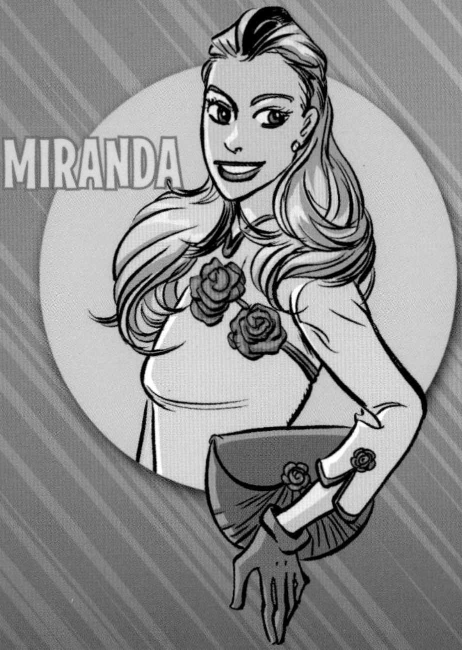
MIRANDA

What are fractions? Fractions are numbers that show parts of a whole. We write fractions with two numbers, one above the other. The top number is the numerator. It tells how many equal parts we have. The bottom number is the denominator. It tells how many equal parts make up 1 whole. When fractions have the same denominator, we can add and subtract them. And we can write 1 whole as any fraction with the same numerator and denominator:

$$\frac{1}{4} + \frac{3}{4} = \frac{1+3}{4} = \frac{4}{4} = 1$$

We use fractions all the time. We use them to divide a pie or a pizza into slices of equal size. We also use them in cooking when a recipe calls for $\frac{1}{2}$ cup or $\frac{1}{4}$ teaspoon. We even use them in telling time!

Story by Melinda Thielbar
Pencils and inks by Tintin Pantoja
Coloring by Hi-Fi Design
Lettering by Marshall Dillon

Graphic Universe™
A division of Lerner Publishing Group, Inc.
241 First Avenue North
Minneapolis, MN 55401 U.S.A.

Website address: www.lernerbooks.com

Library of Congress Cataloging-in-Publication Data

Thielbar, Melinda.
        The ancient formula : a mystery with fractions / by Melinda Thielbar ;
    illustrated by Tintin Pantoja.
            p.   cm. — (Manga math mysteries ; #5)
        Summary: The students of Sifu Faiza's Kung Fu School use their knowledge of
    fractions as they try to discover what happened to Leung Jan's long-lost healing
    formula.
        ISBN: 978–0–7613–4907–5 (lib. bdg. : alk. paper)
        1. Graphic novels. [1. Graphic novels. 2. Mystery and detective stories.
    3. Mathematics—Fiction. 4. Kung fu—Fiction. 5. Schools—Fiction.] I. Pantoja,
    Tintin, ill. II. Title.
    PZ7.7.T48Anc 2011
    741.5'973—dc22   2010001431

Manufactured in the United States of America
2 – DP – 7/1/11

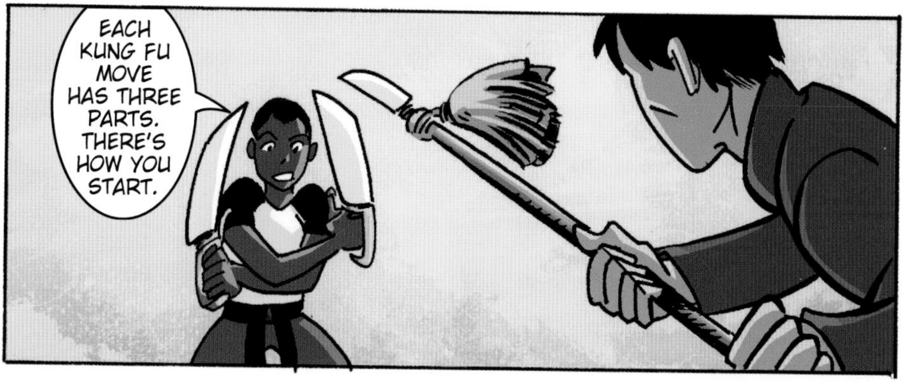
EACH KUNG FU MOVE HAS THREE PARTS. THERE'S HOW YOU START.
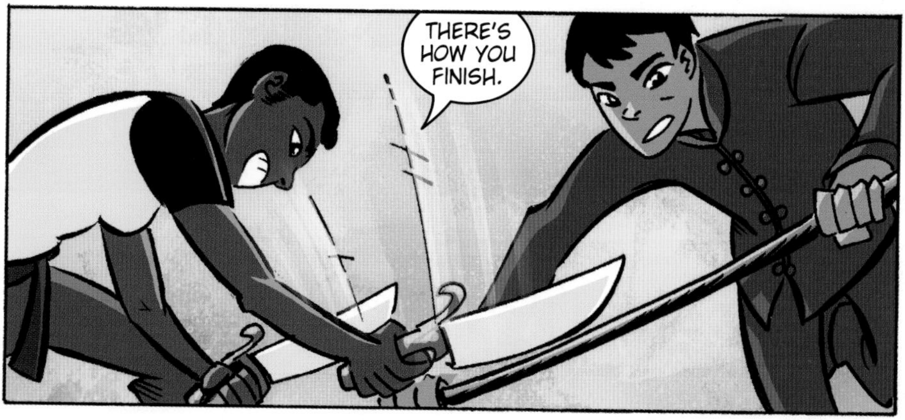
THERE'S HOW YOU FINISH.
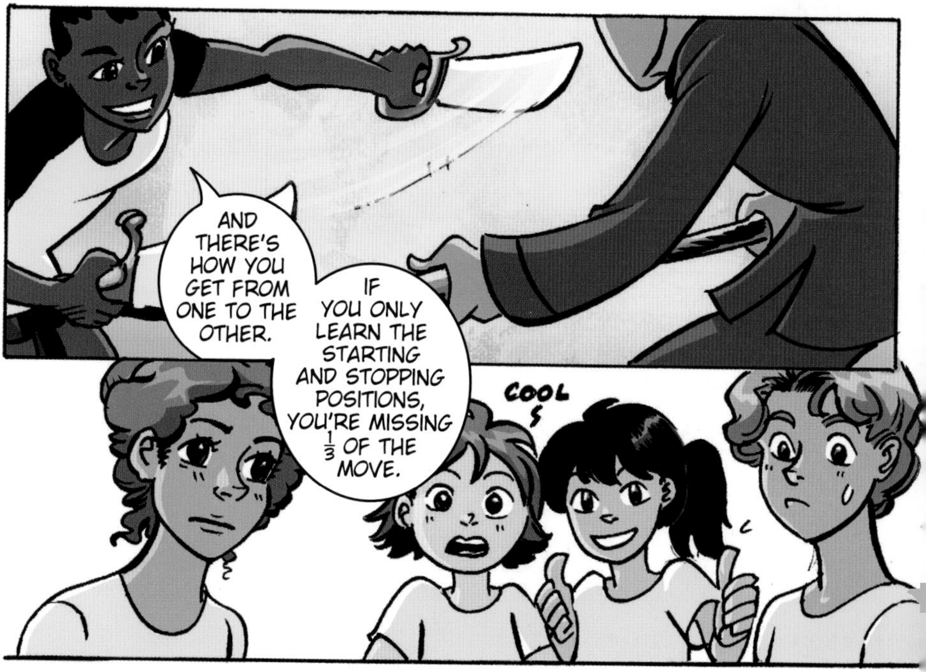
AND THERE'S HOW YOU GET FROM ONE TO THE OTHER.
IF YOU ONLY LEARN THE STARTING AND STOPPING POSITIONS, YOU'RE MISSING 1/3 OF THE MOVE.
COOL

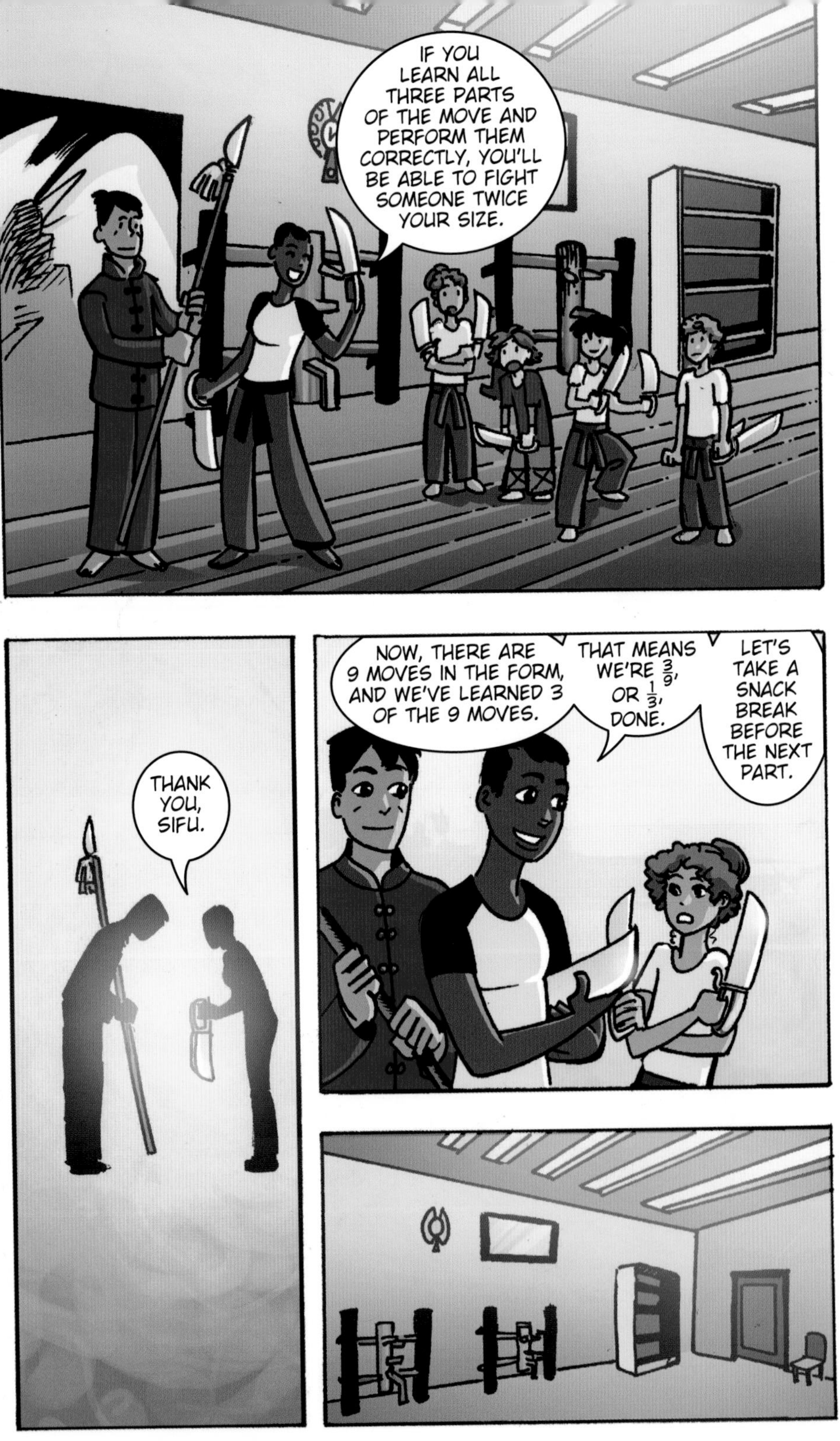
IF YOU LEARN ALL THREE PARTS OF THE MOVE AND PERFORM THEM CORRECTLY, YOU'LL BE ABLE TO FIGHT SOMEONE TWICE YOUR SIZE.
THANK YOU, SIFU.
NOW, THERE ARE 9 MOVES IN THE FORM, AND WE'VE LEARNED 3 OF THE 9 MOVES.
THAT MEANS WE'RE $\frac{3}{9}$, OR $\frac{1}{3}$, DONE.
LET'S TAKE A SNACK BREAK BEFORE THE NEXT PART.

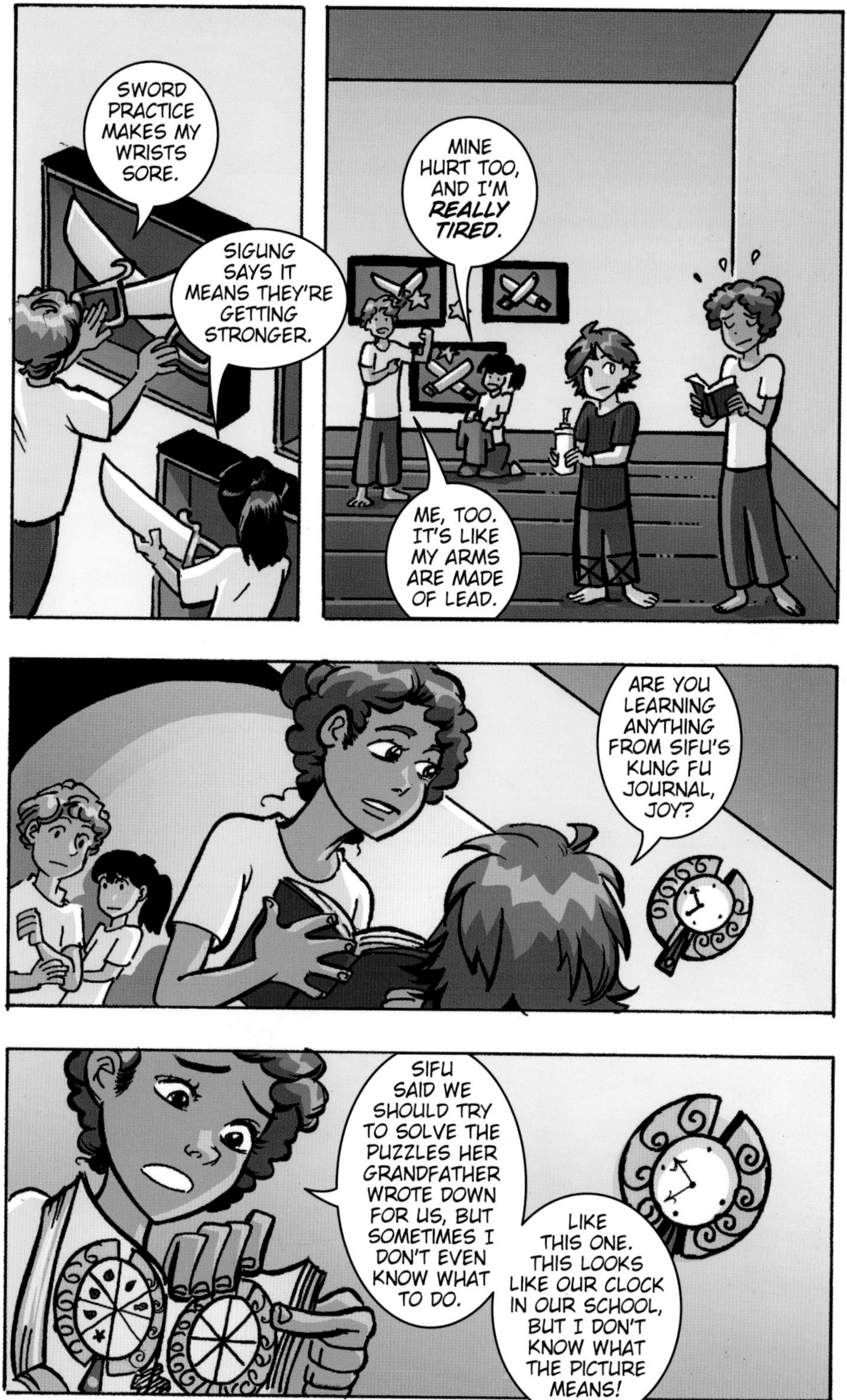
SWORD PRACTICE MAKES MY WRISTS SORE.
SIGUNG SAYS IT MEANS THEY'RE GETTING STRONGER.
MINE HURT TOO, AND I'M ***REALLY TIRED***.
ME, TOO. IT'S LIKE MY ARMS ARE MADE OF LEAD.
ARE YOU LEARNING ANYTHING FROM SIFU'S KUNG FU JOURNAL, JOY?
SIFU SAID WE SHOULD TRY TO SOLVE THE PUZZLES HER GRANDFATHER WROTE DOWN FOR US, BUT SOMETIMES I DON'T EVEN KNOW WHAT TO DO.
LIKE THIS ONE. THIS LOOKS LIKE OUR CLOCK IN OUR SCHOOL, BUT I DON'T KNOW WHAT THE PICTURE MEANS!

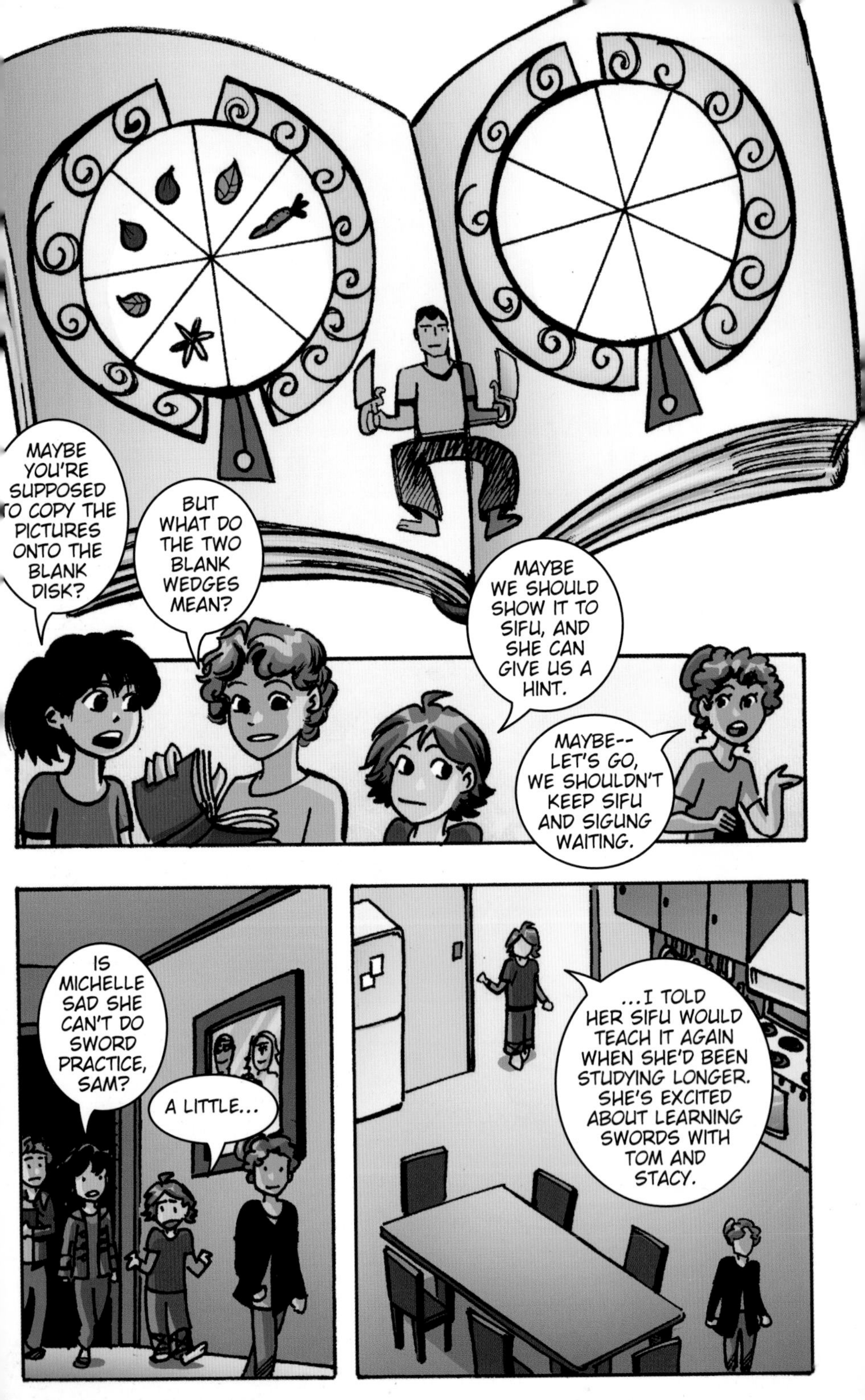
MAYBE YOU'RE SUPPOSED TO COPY THE PICTURES ONTO THE BLANK DISK?
BUT WHAT DO THE TWO BLANK WEDGES MEAN?
MAYBE WE SHOULD SHOW IT TO SIFU, AND SHE CAN GIVE US A HINT.
MAYBE-- LET'S GO, WE SHOULDN'T KEEP SIFU AND SIGUNG WAITING.
IS MICHELLE SAD SHE CAN'T DO SWORD PRACTICE, SAM?
A LITTLE...
...I TOLD HER SIFU WOULD TEACH IT AGAIN WHEN SHE'D BEEN STUDYING LONGER. SHE'S EXCITED ABOUT LEARNING SWORDS WITH TOM AND STACY.

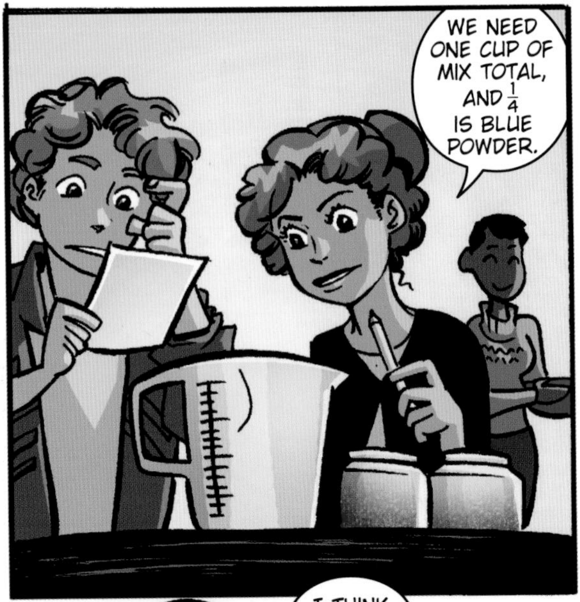
WE NEED ONE CUP OF MIX TOTAL, AND $\frac{1}{4}$ IS BLUE POWDER.

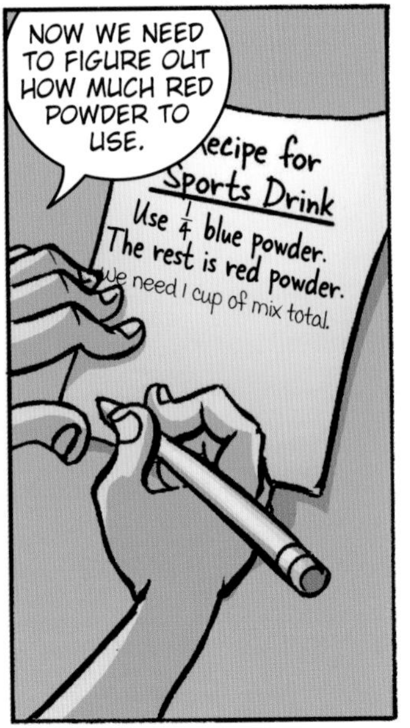
NOW WE NEED TO FIGURE OUT HOW MUCH RED POWDER TO USE.
Sports Drink
Use $\frac{1}{4}$ blue powder.
The rest is red powder.
We need 1 cup of mix total.

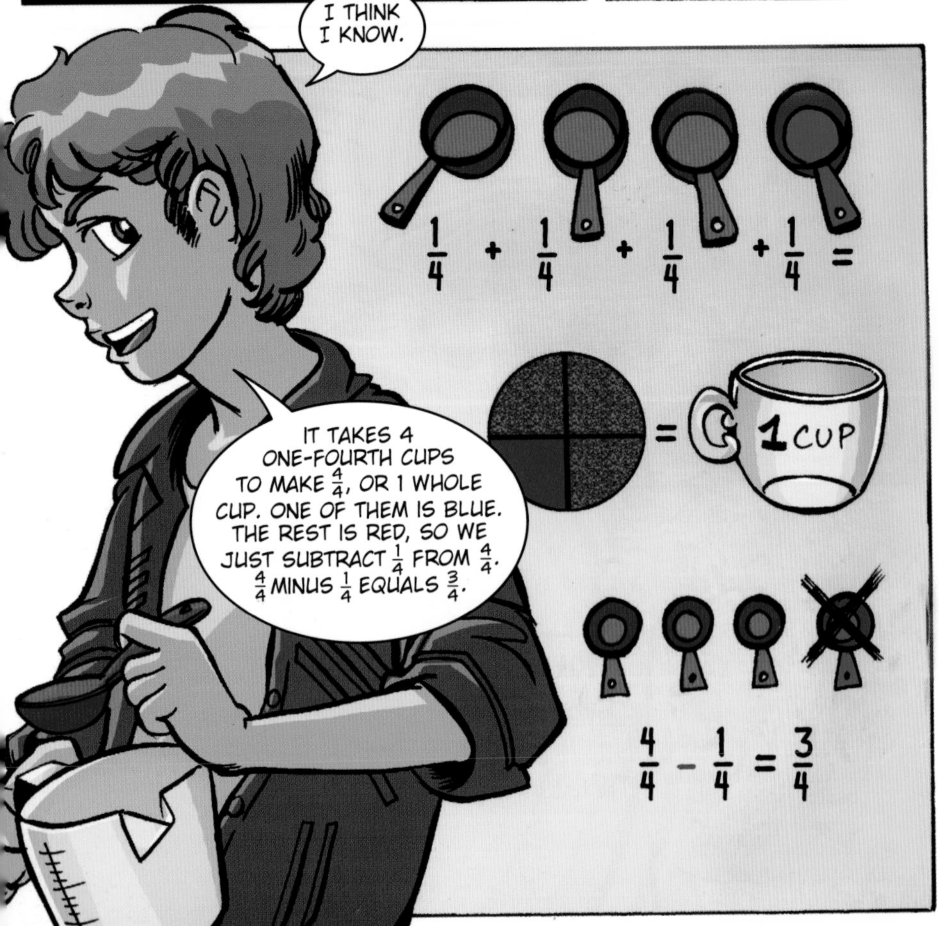
I THINK I KNOW.
$\frac{1}{4} + \frac{1}{4} + \frac{1}{4} + \frac{1}{4} =$
= 1 CUP
IT TAKES 4 ONE-FOURTH CUPS TO MAKE $\frac{4}{4}$, OR 1 WHOLE CUP. ONE OF THEM IS BLUE. THE REST IS RED, SO WE JUST SUBTRACT $\frac{1}{4}$ FROM $\frac{4}{4}$. $\frac{4}{4}$ MINUS $\frac{1}{4}$ EQUALS $\frac{3}{4}$.
$\frac{4}{4} - \frac{1}{4} = \frac{3}{4}$

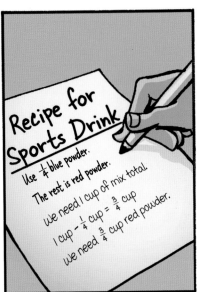

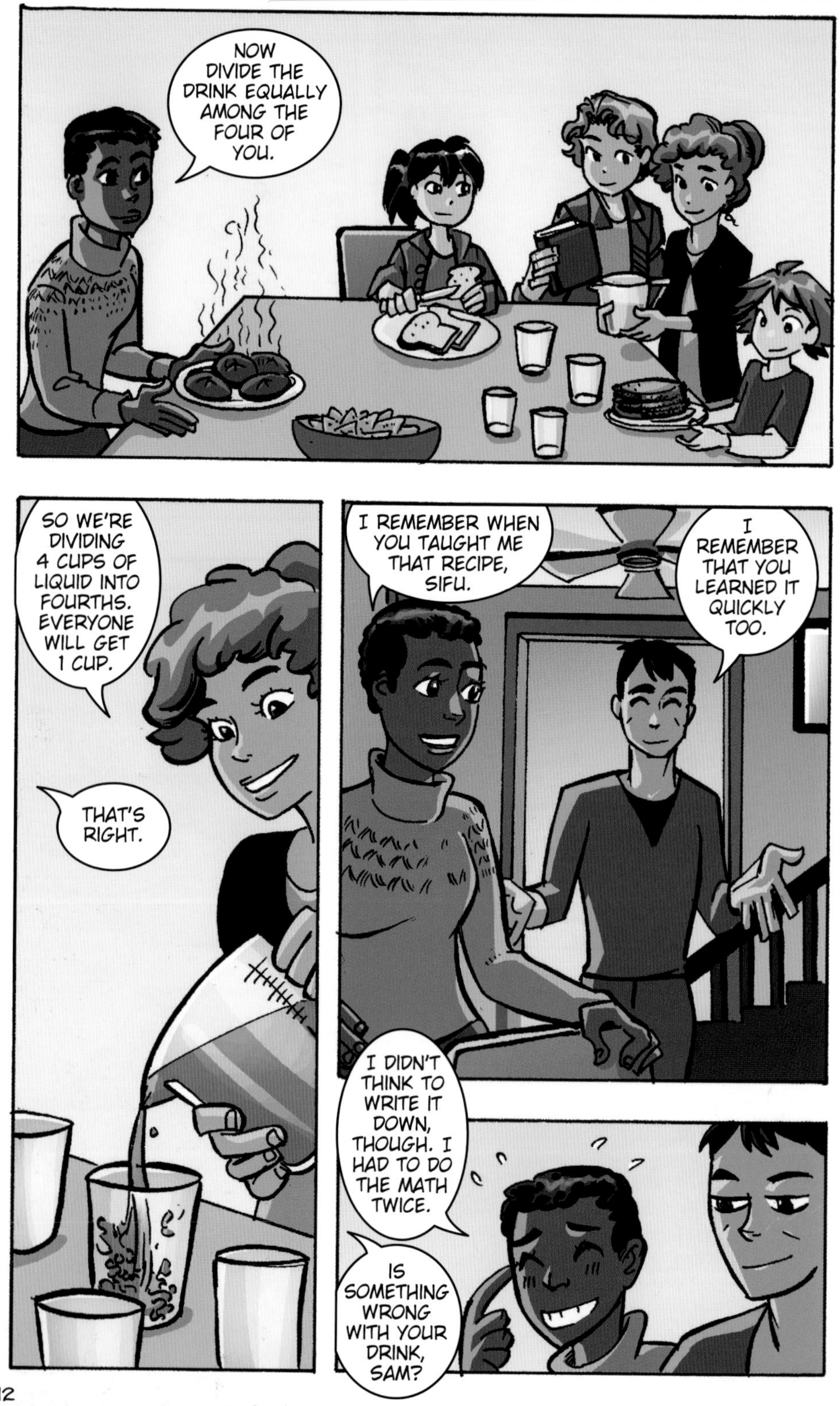
NOW DIVIDE THE DRINK EQUALLY AMONG THE FOUR OF YOU.
SO WE'RE DIVIDING 4 CUPS OF LIQUID INTO FOURTHS. EVERYONE WILL GET 1 CUP.
THAT'S RIGHT.
I REMEMBER WHEN YOU TAUGHT ME THAT RECIPE, SIFU.
I REMEMBER THAT YOU LEARNED IT QUICKLY TOO.
I DIDN'T THINK TO WRITE IT DOWN, THOUGH. I HAD TO DO THE MATH TWICE.
IS SOMETHING WRONG WITH YOUR DRINK, SAM?

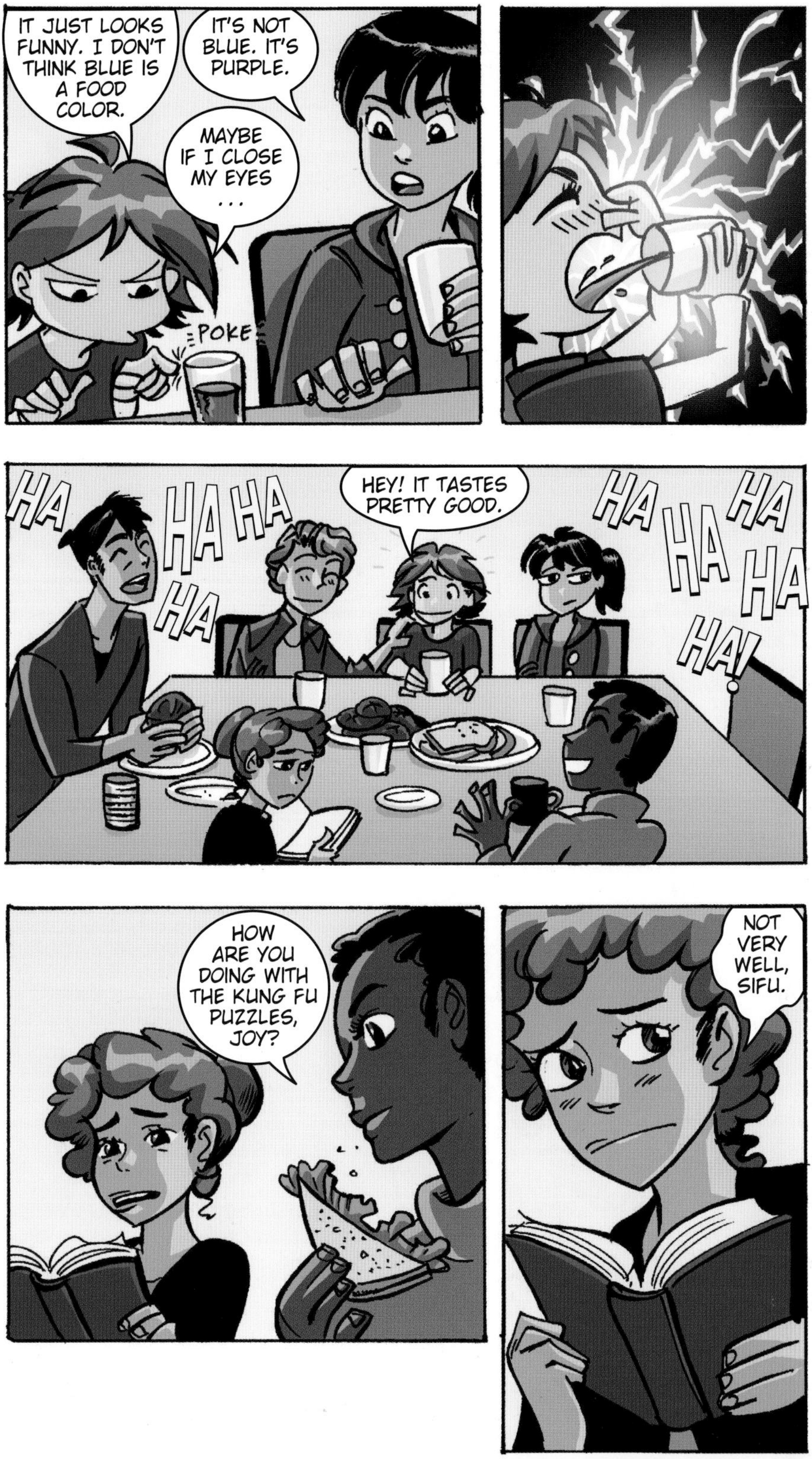
IT JUST LOOKS FUNNY. I DON'T THINK BLUE IS A FOOD COLOR.
IT'S NOT BLUE. IT'S PURPLE.
MAYBE IF I CLOSE MY EYES . . .
POKE
HA
HA HA
HA
HEY! IT TASTES PRETTY GOOD.
HA HA HA HA HA HA!
HOW ARE YOU DOING WITH THE KUNG FU PUZZLES, JOY?
NOT VERY WELL, SIFU.

14

--BUT YOU WOULD BOW VERY DEEPLY WHEN YOU SAY IT.
SIFU LEUNG JAN WAS A GREAT KUNG FU MASTER.
HE WAS ALSO A DOCTOR.
HE INVENTED A SPECIAL KIND OF JOW--CHINESE MEDICINE FOR KUNG FU STUDENTS.
SIFU LEUNG'S MEDICINE WAS THE BEST.

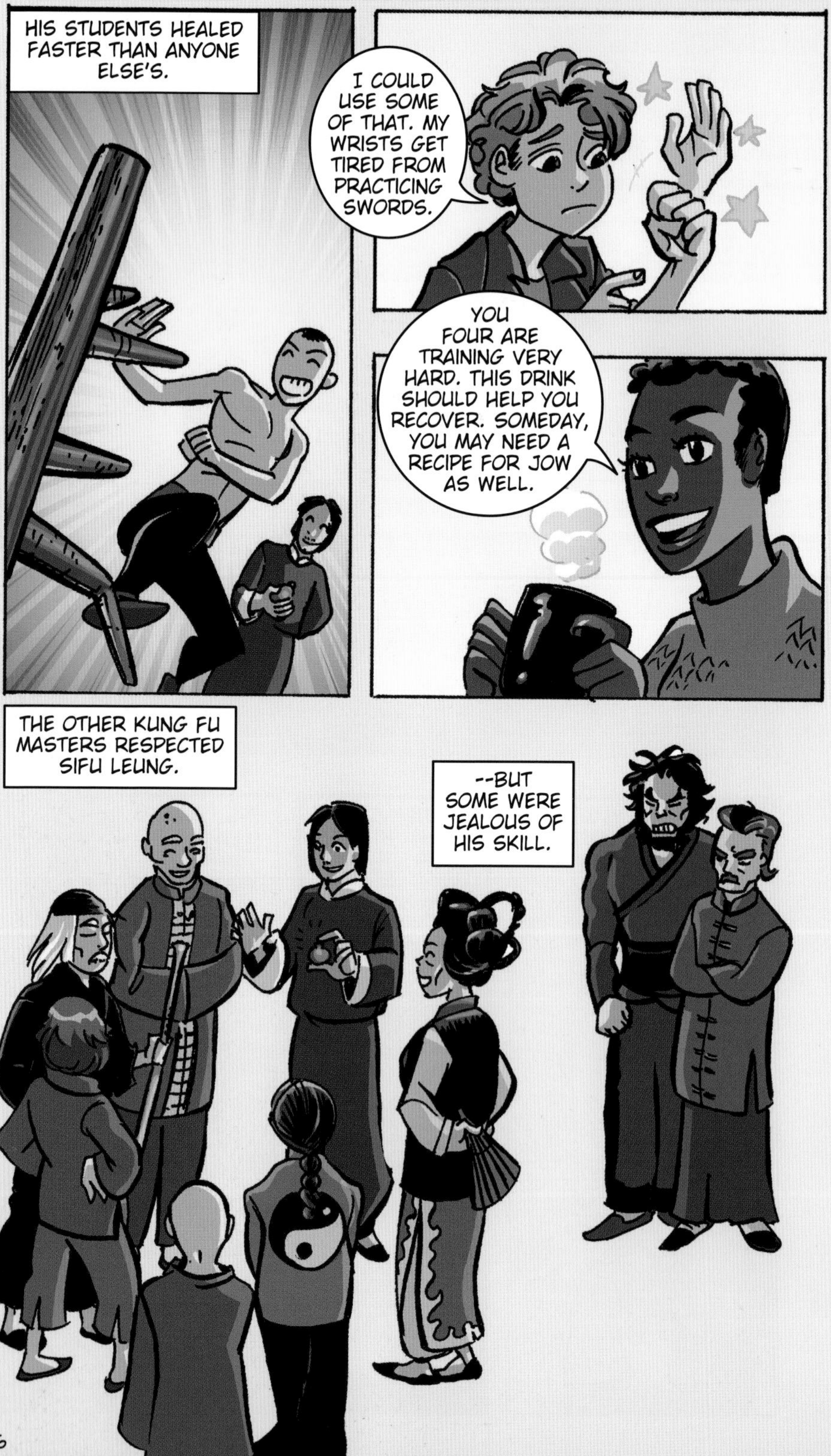
HIS STUDENTS HEALED FASTER THAN ANYONE ELSE'S.
I COULD USE SOME OF THAT. MY WRISTS GET TIRED FROM PRACTICING SWORDS.
YOU FOUR ARE TRAINING VERY HARD. THIS DRINK SHOULD HELP YOU RECOVER. SOMEDAY, YOU MAY NEED A RECIPE FOR JOW AS WELL.
THE OTHER KUNG FU MASTERS RESPECTED SIFU LEUNG.
--BUT SOME WERE JEALOUS OF HIS SKILL.

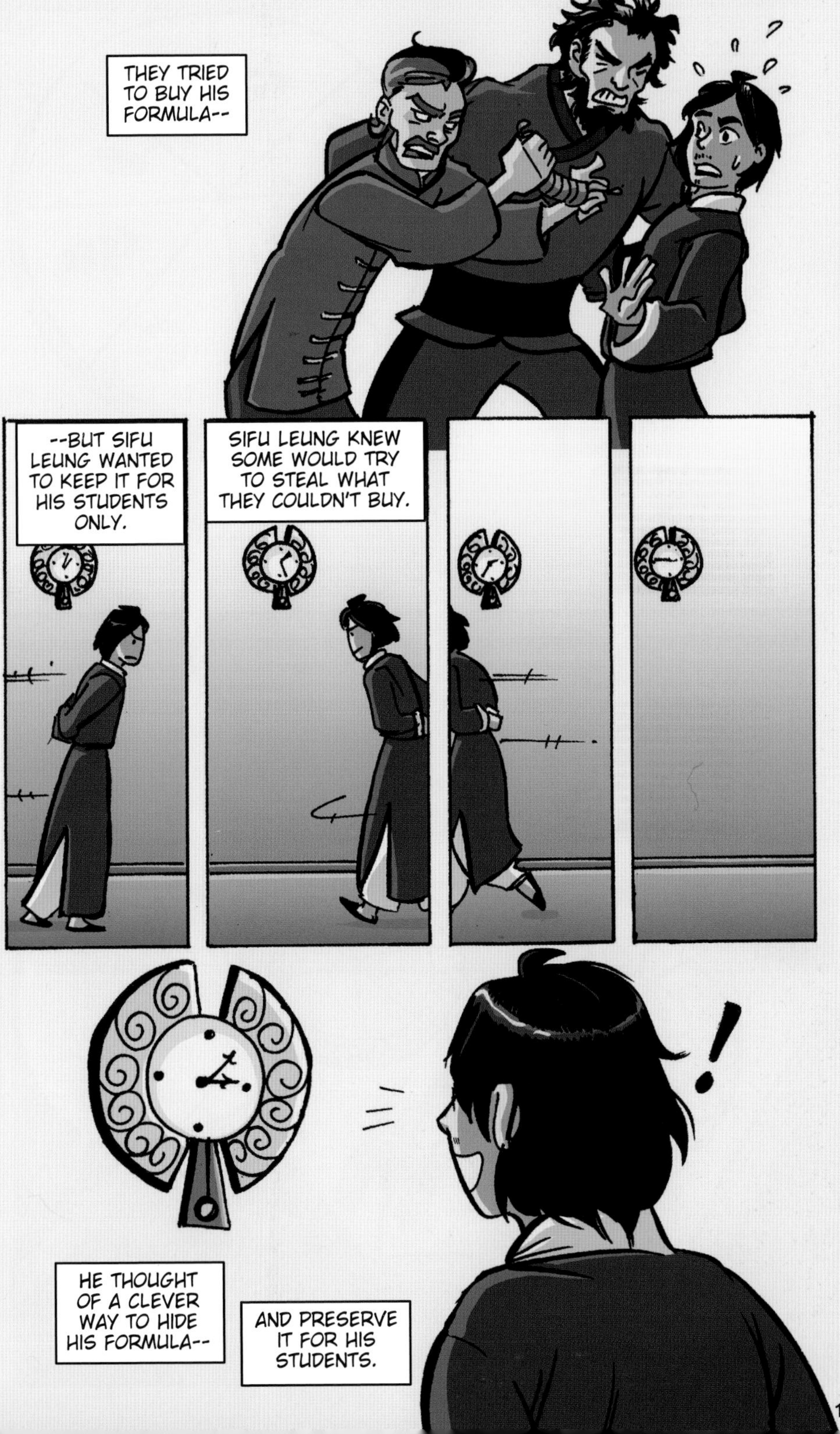

THEY TRIED TO BUY HIS FORMULA--
--BUT SIFU LEUNG WANTED TO KEEP IT FOR HIS STUDENTS ONLY.
SIFU LEUNG KNEW SOME WOULD TRY TO STEAL WHAT THEY COULDN'T BUY.
!
HE THOUGHT OF A CLEVER WAY TO HIDE HIS FORMULA--
AND PRESERVE IT FOR HIS STUDENTS.

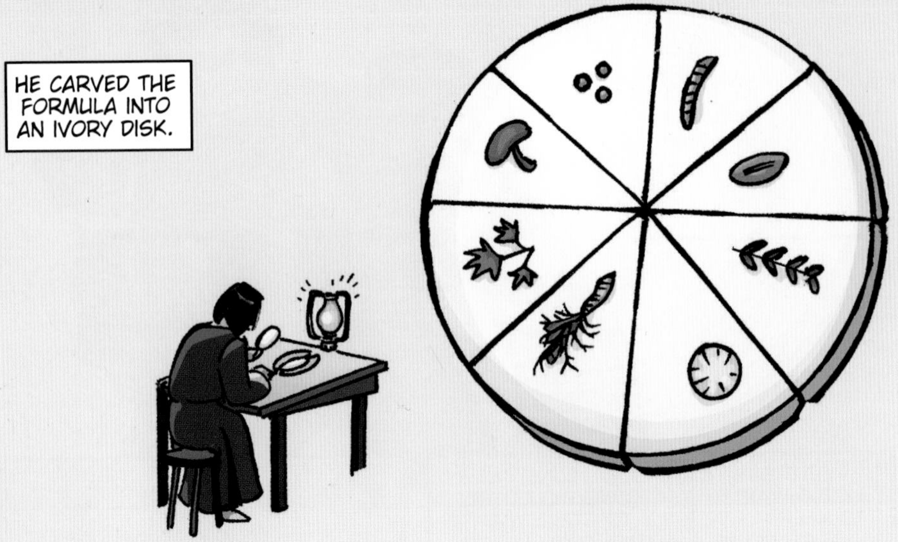
HE CARVED THE FORMULA INTO AN IVORY DISK.

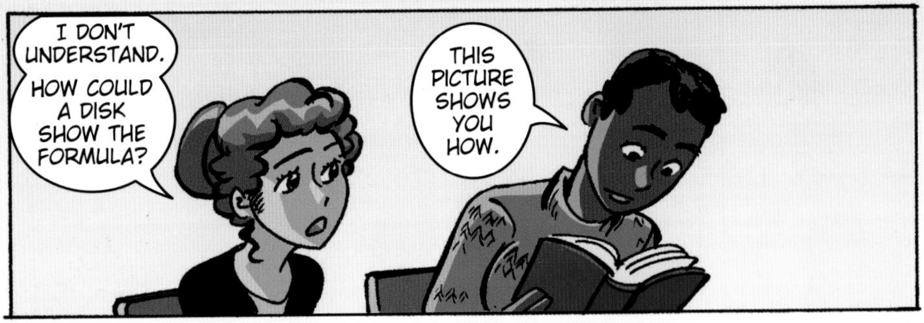
I DON'T UNDERSTAND.
HOW COULD A DISK SHOW THE FORMULA?
THIS PICTURE SHOWS YOU HOW.

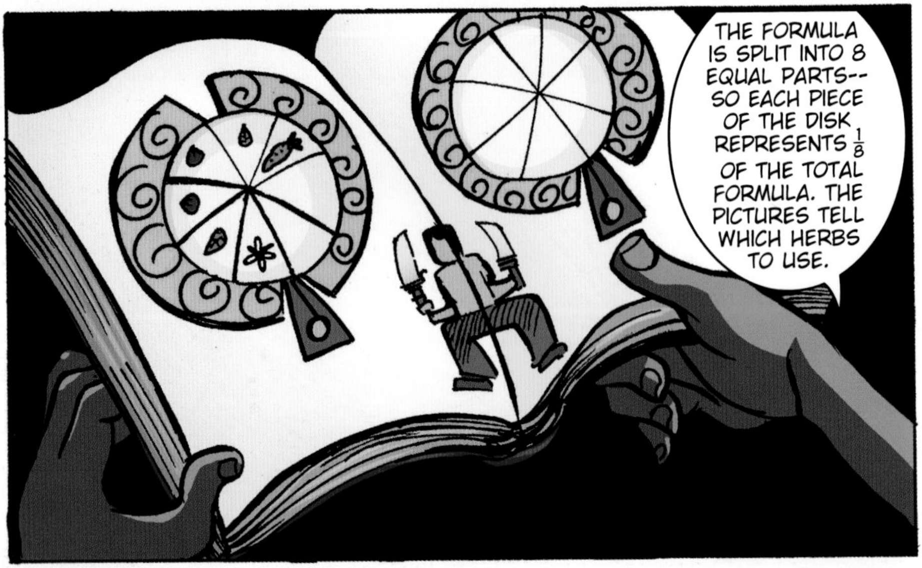
THE FORMULA IS SPLIT INTO 8 EQUAL PARTS-- SO EACH PIECE OF THE DISK REPRESENTS $\frac{1}{8}$ OF THE TOTAL FORMULA. THE PICTURES TELL WHICH HERBS TO USE.

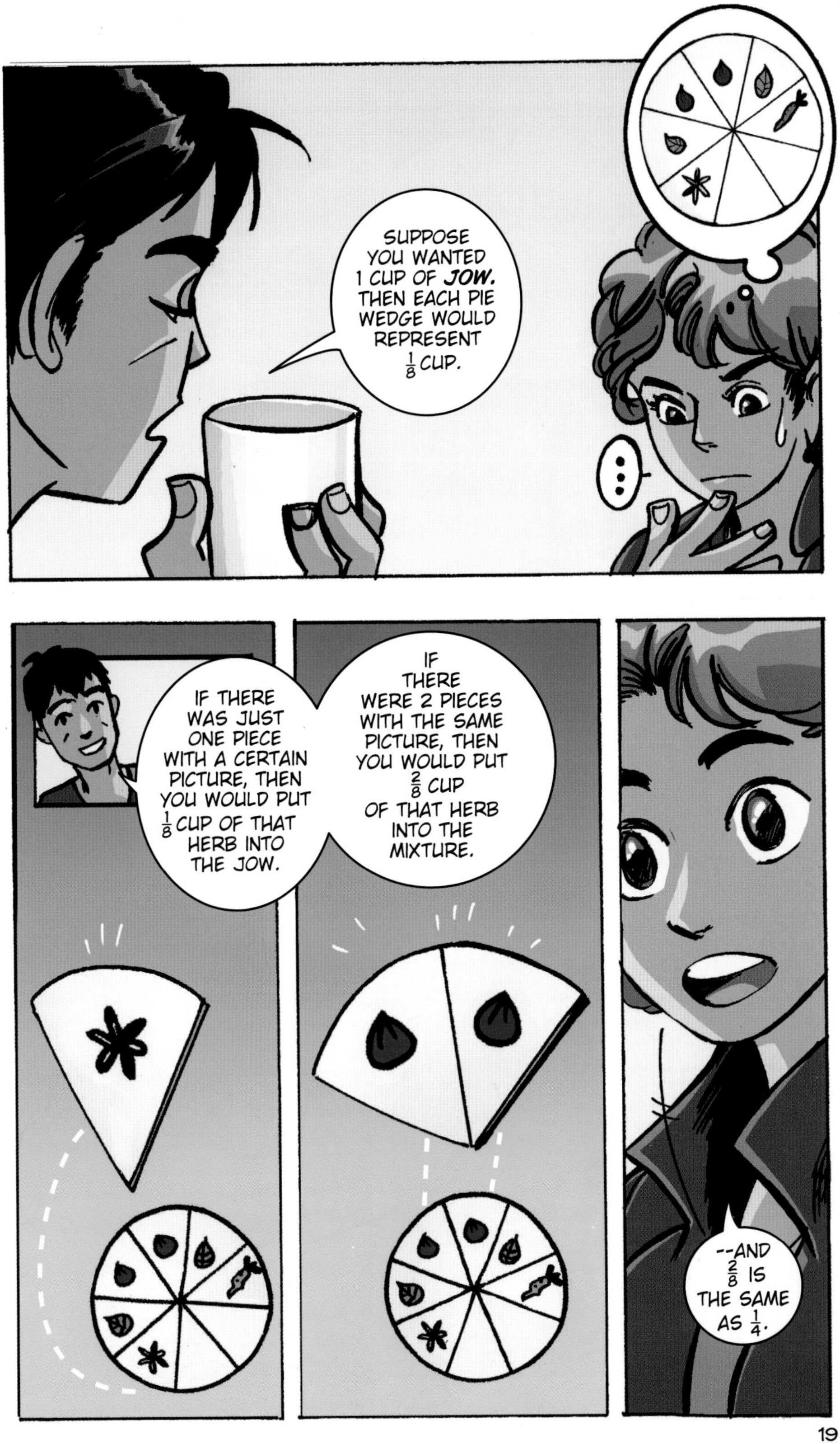
SUPPOSE YOU WANTED 1 CUP OF ***JOW.*** THEN EACH PIE WEDGE WOULD REPRESENT $\frac{1}{8}$ CUP.
...
IF THERE WAS JUST ONE PIECE WITH A CERTAIN PICTURE, THEN YOU WOULD PUT $\frac{1}{8}$ CUP OF THAT HERB INTO THE JOW.
IF THERE WERE 2 PIECES WITH THE SAME PICTURE, THEN YOU WOULD PUT $\frac{2}{8}$ CUP OF THAT HERB INTO THE MIXTURE.
--AND $\frac{2}{8}$ IS THE SAME AS $\frac{1}{4}$.

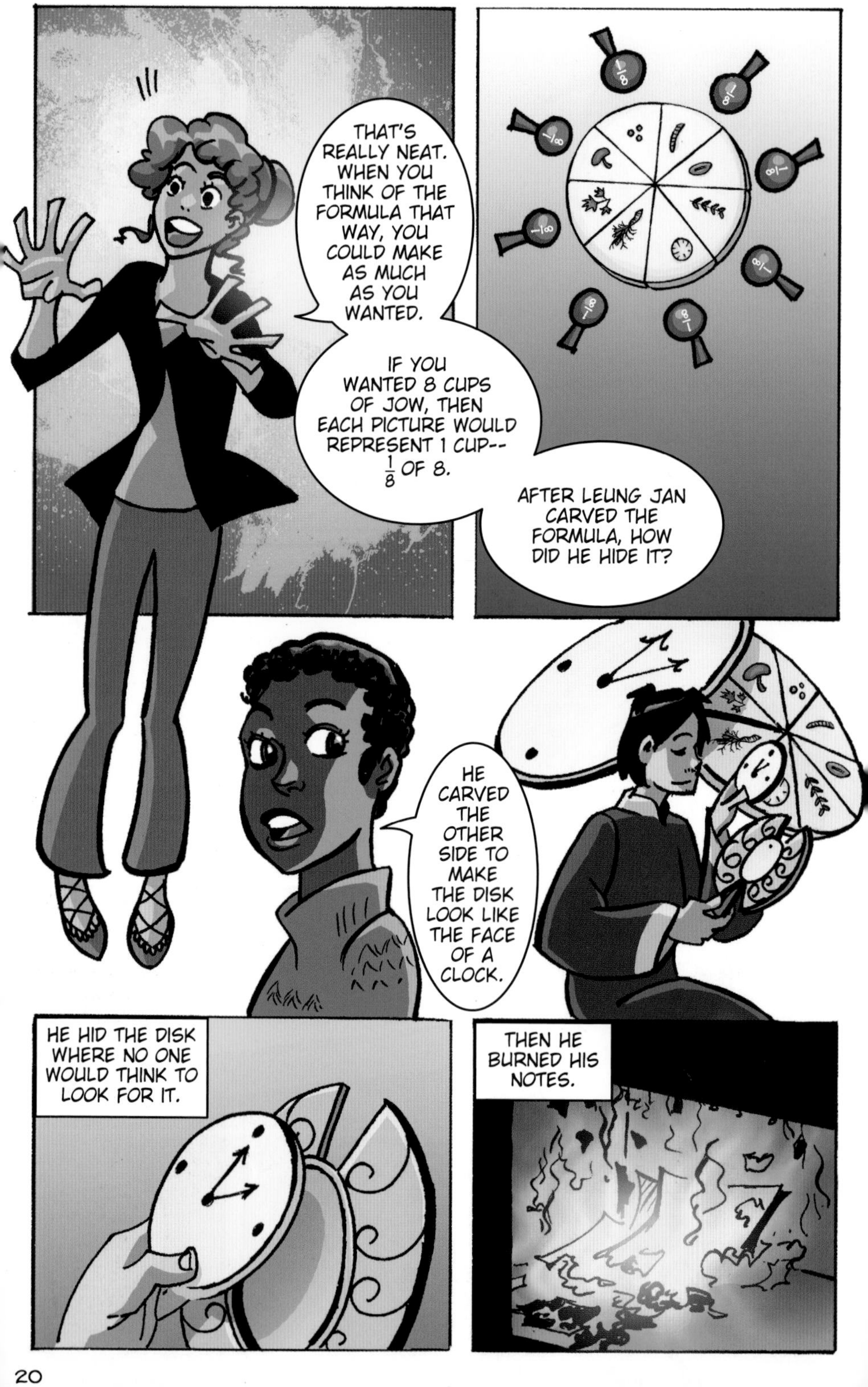
THAT'S REALLY NEAT. WHEN YOU THINK OF THE FORMULA THAT WAY, YOU COULD MAKE AS MUCH AS YOU WANTED.
IF YOU WANTED 8 CUPS OF JOW, THEN EACH PICTURE WOULD REPRESENT 1 CUP-- $\frac{1}{8}$ OF 8.
AFTER LEUNG JAN CARVED THE FORMULA, HOW DID HE HIDE IT?
HE CARVED THE OTHER SIDE TO MAKE THE DISK LOOK LIKE THE FACE OF A CLOCK.
HE HID THE DISK WHERE NO ONE WOULD THINK TO LOOK FOR IT.
THEN HE BURNED HIS NOTES.

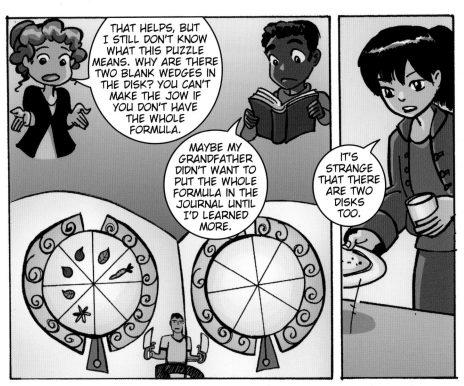

22

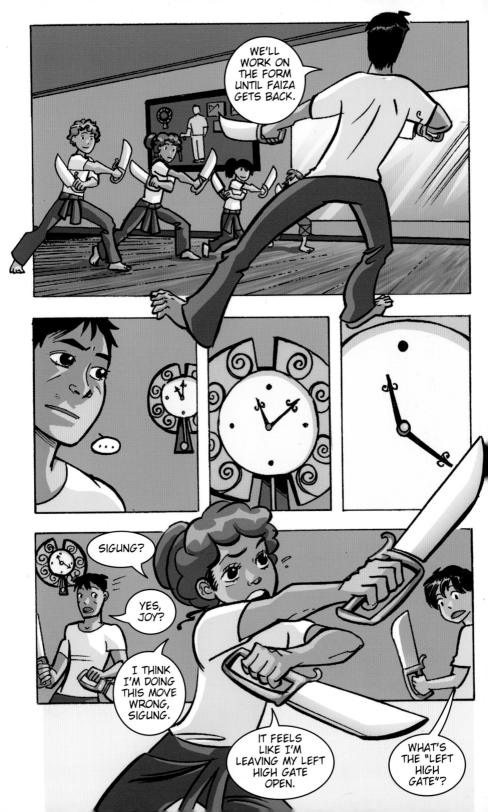

24

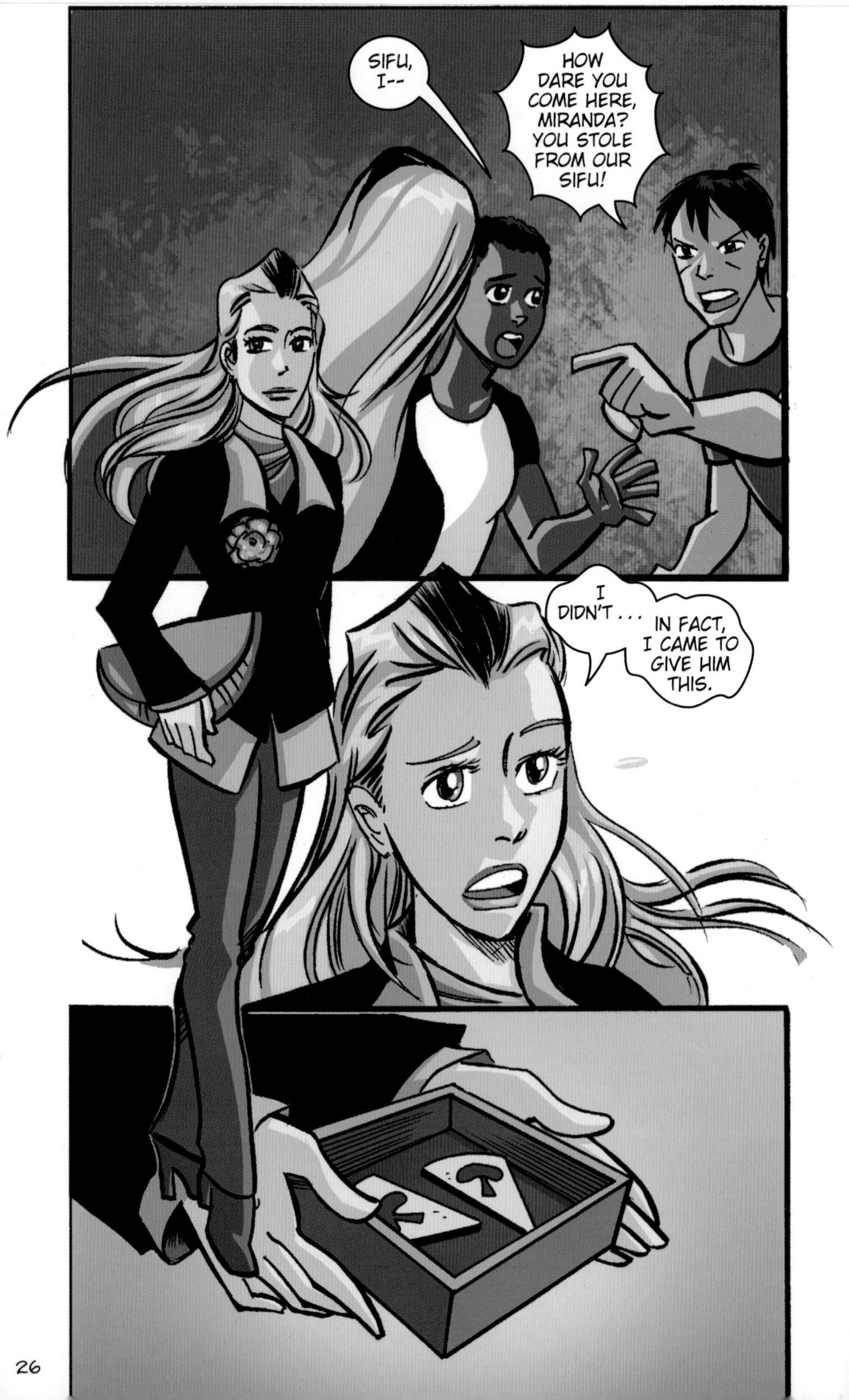
SIFU, I--
HOW DARE YOU COME HERE, MIRANDA? YOU STOLE FROM OUR SIFU!
I DIDN'T . . .
IN FACT, I CAME TO GIVE HIM THIS.

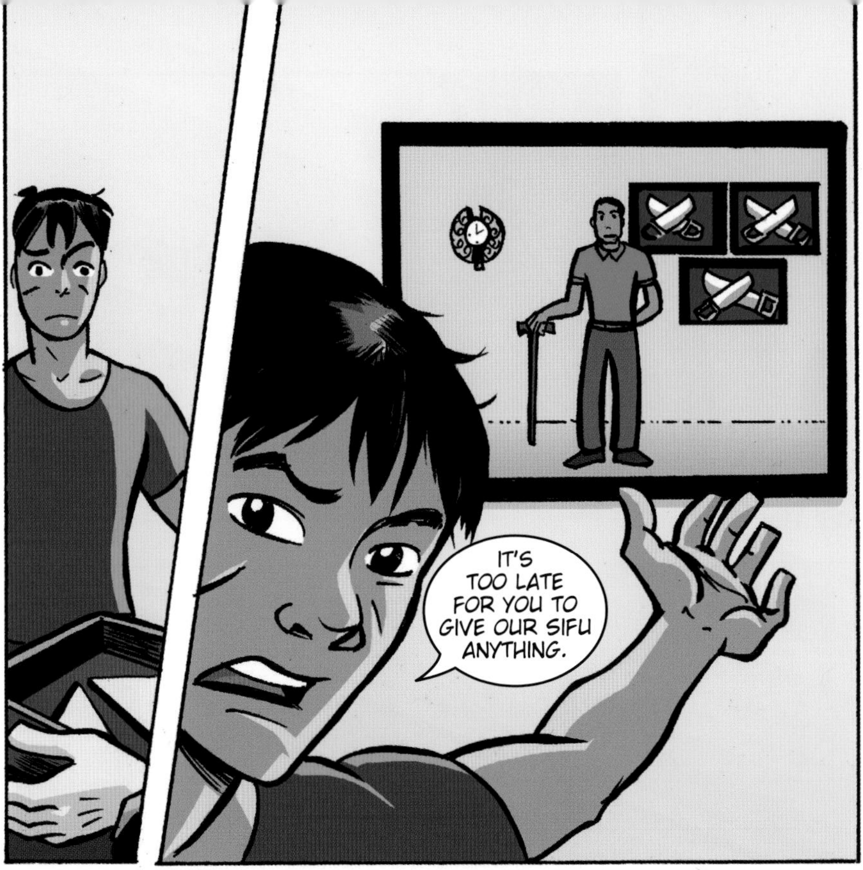
IT'S TOO LATE FOR YOU TO GIVE OUR SIFU ANYTHING.

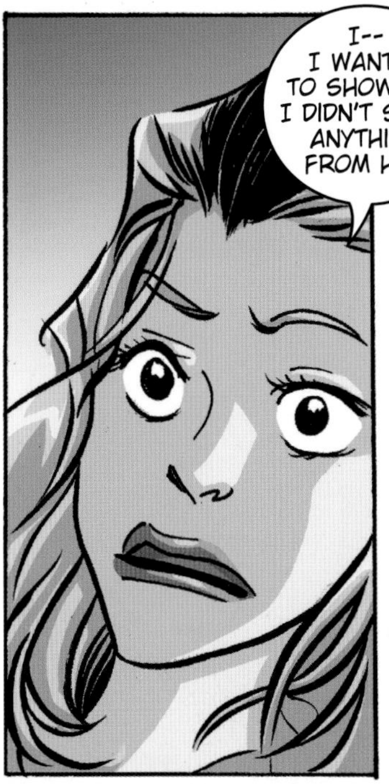
I-- I WANTED TO SHOW HIM I DIDN'T STEAL ANYTHING FROM HIM.

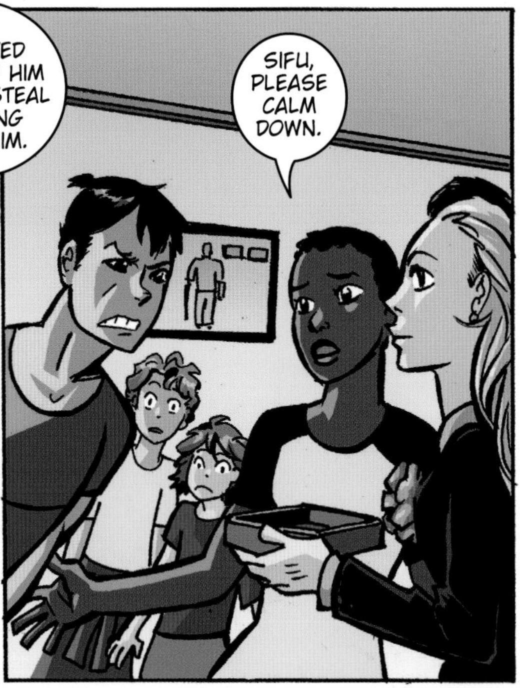
SIFU, PLEASE CALM DOWN.

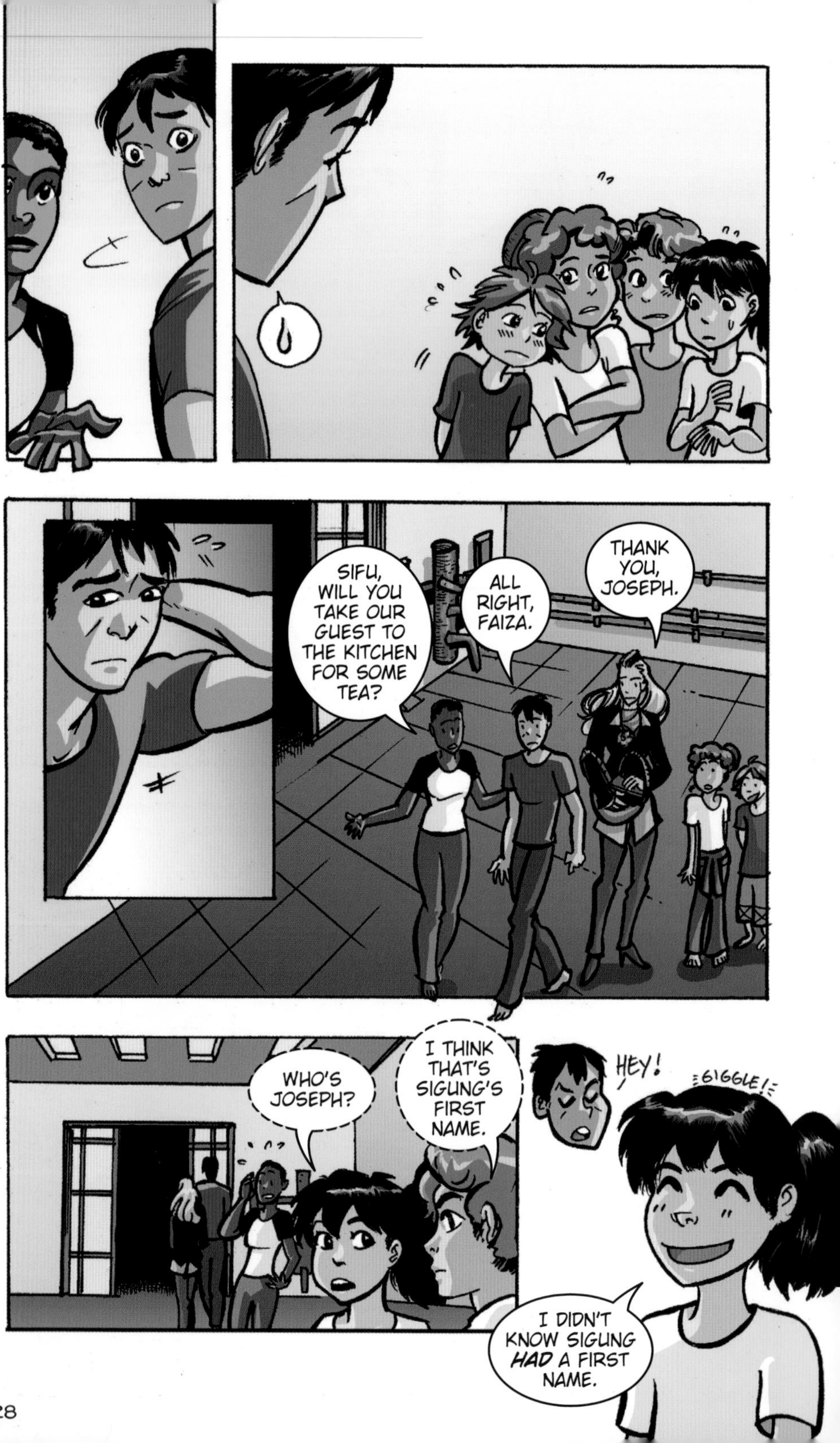
SIFU, WILL YOU TAKE OUR GUEST TO THE KITCHEN FOR SOME TEA?
ALL RIGHT, FAIZA.
THANK YOU, JOSEPH.
WHO'S JOSEPH?
I THINK THAT'S SIGUNG'S FIRST NAME.
HEY!
GIGGLE!
I DIDN'T KNOW SIGUNG HAD A FIRST NAME.

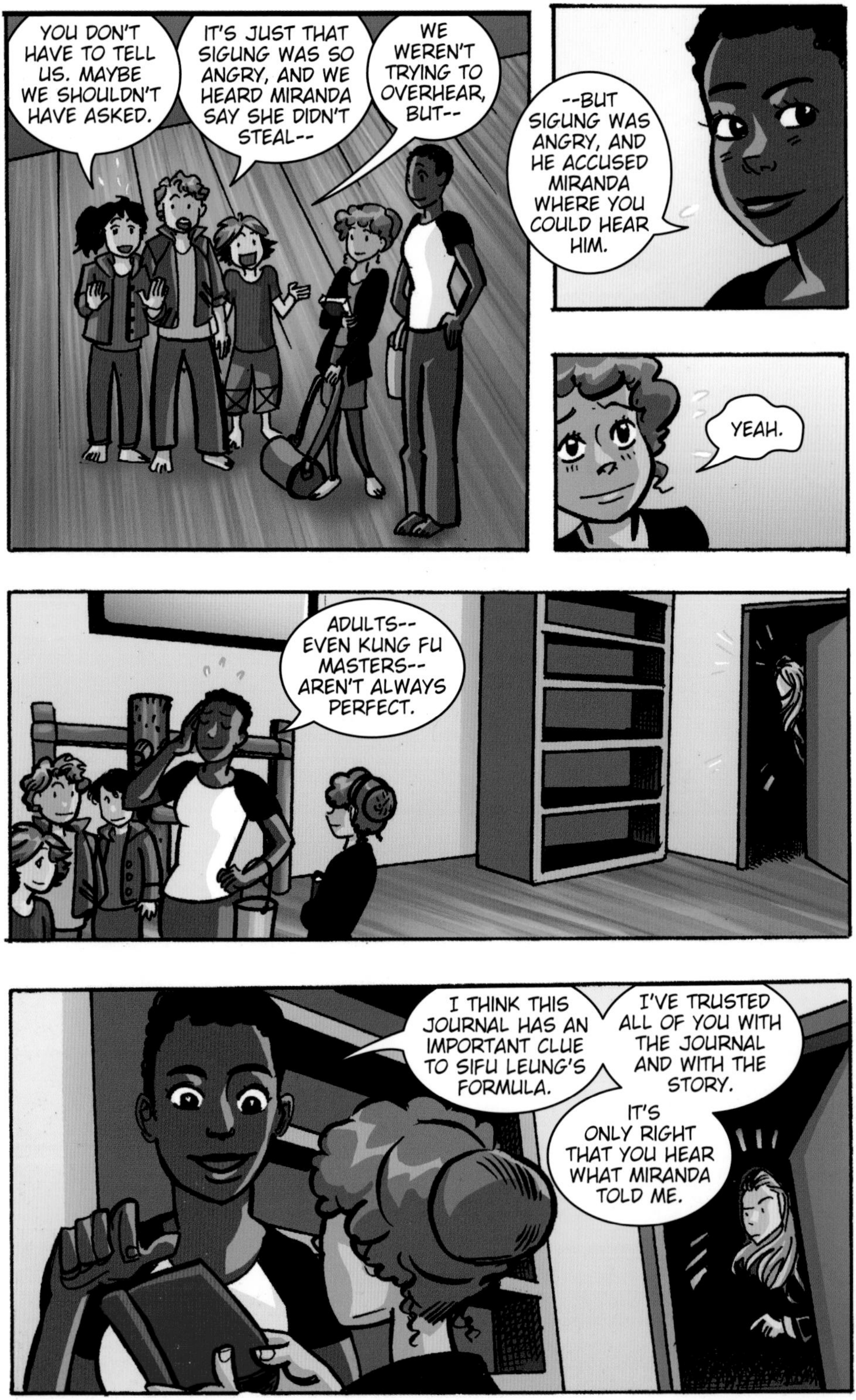
YOU DON'T HAVE TO TELL US. MAYBE WE SHOULDN'T HAVE ASKED.
IT'S JUST THAT SIGUNG WAS SO ANGRY, AND WE HEARD MIRANDA SAY SHE DIDN'T STEAL--
WE WEREN'T TRYING TO OVERHEAR, BUT--
--BUT SIGUNG WAS ANGRY, AND HE ACCUSED MIRANDA WHERE YOU COULD HEAR HIM.
YEAH.
ADULTS--EVEN KUNG FU MASTERS--AREN'T ALWAYS PERFECT.
I THINK THIS JOURNAL HAS AN IMPORTANT CLUE TO SIFU LEUNG'S FORMULA.
I'VE TRUSTED ALL OF YOU WITH THE JOURNAL AND WITH THE STORY.
IT'S ONLY RIGHT THAT YOU HEAR WHAT MIRANDA TOLD ME.

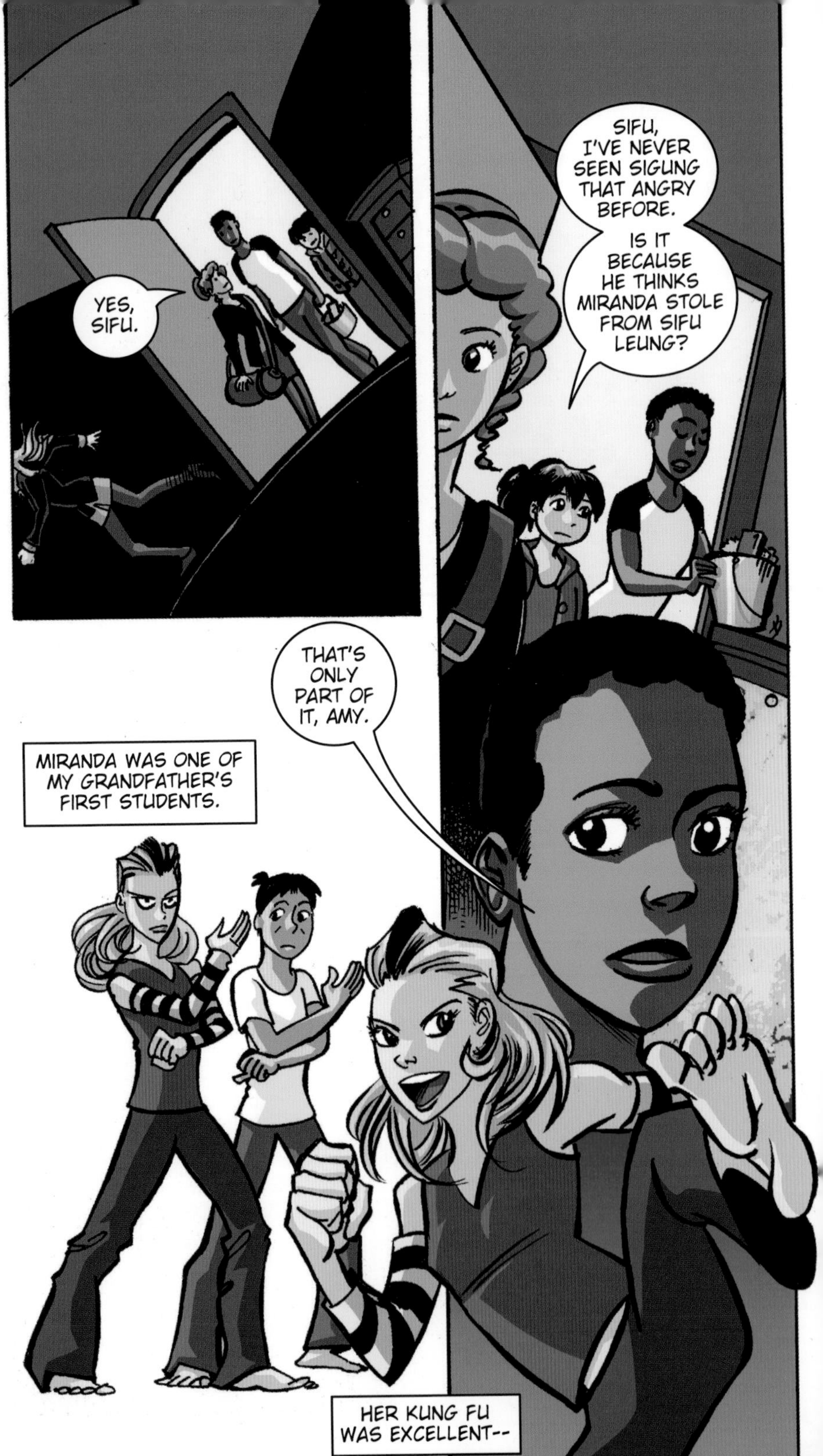
YES, SIFU.
SIFU, I'VE NEVER SEEN SIGUNG THAT ANGRY BEFORE.
IS IT BECAUSE HE THINKS MIRANDA STOLE FROM SIFU LEUNG?
THAT'S ONLY PART OF IT, AMY.
MIRANDA WAS ONE OF MY GRANDFATHER'S FIRST STUDENTS.
HER KUNG FU WAS EXCELLENT--

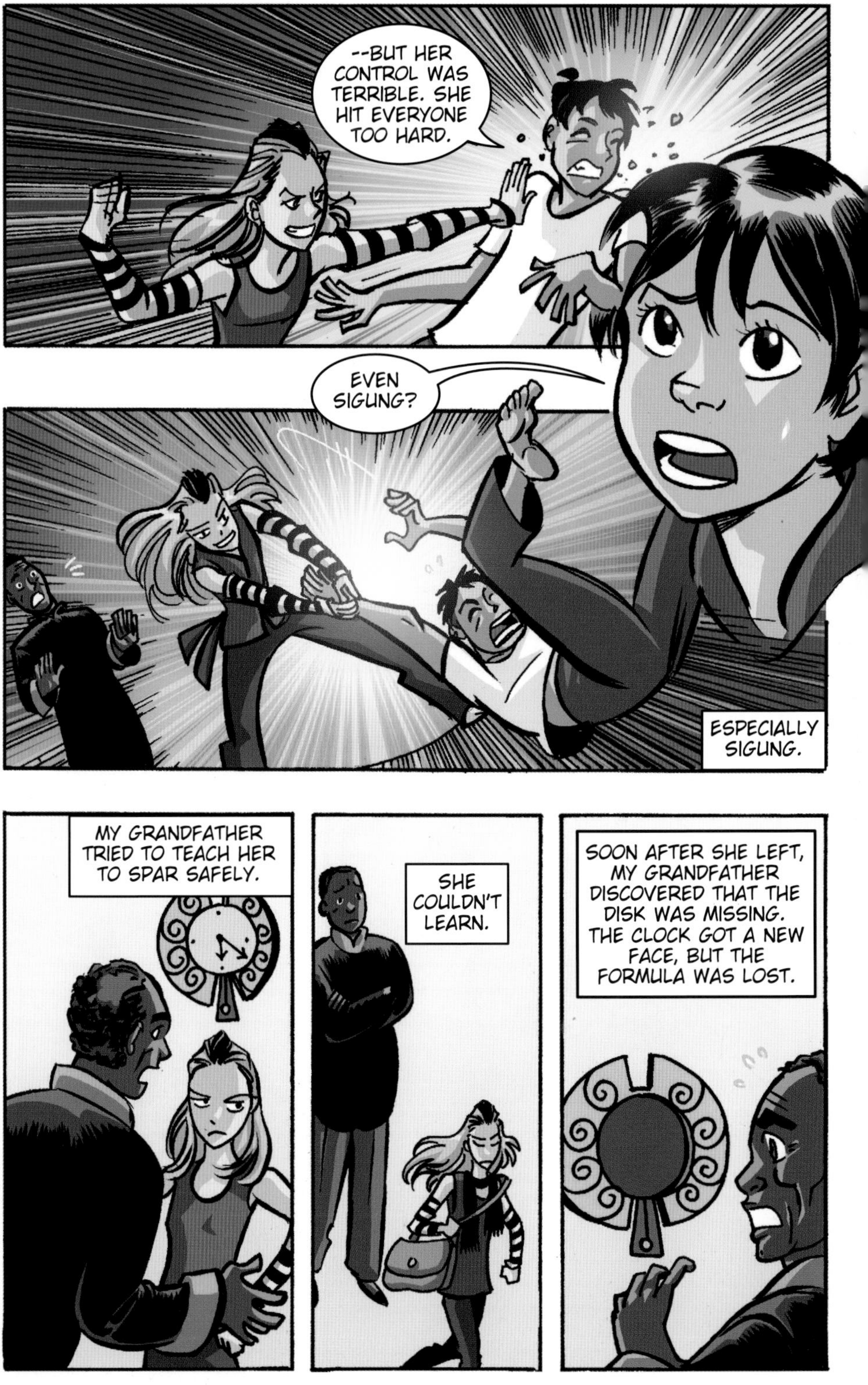
--BUT HER CONTROL WAS TERRIBLE. SHE HIT EVERYONE TOO HARD.
EVEN SIGUNG?
ESPECIALLY SIGUNG.
MY GRANDFATHER TRIED TO TEACH HER TO SPAR SAFELY.
SHE COULDN'T LEARN.
SOON AFTER SHE LEFT, MY GRANDFATHER DISCOVERED THAT THE DISK WAS MISSING. THE CLOCK GOT A NEW FACE, BUT THE FORMULA WAS LOST.

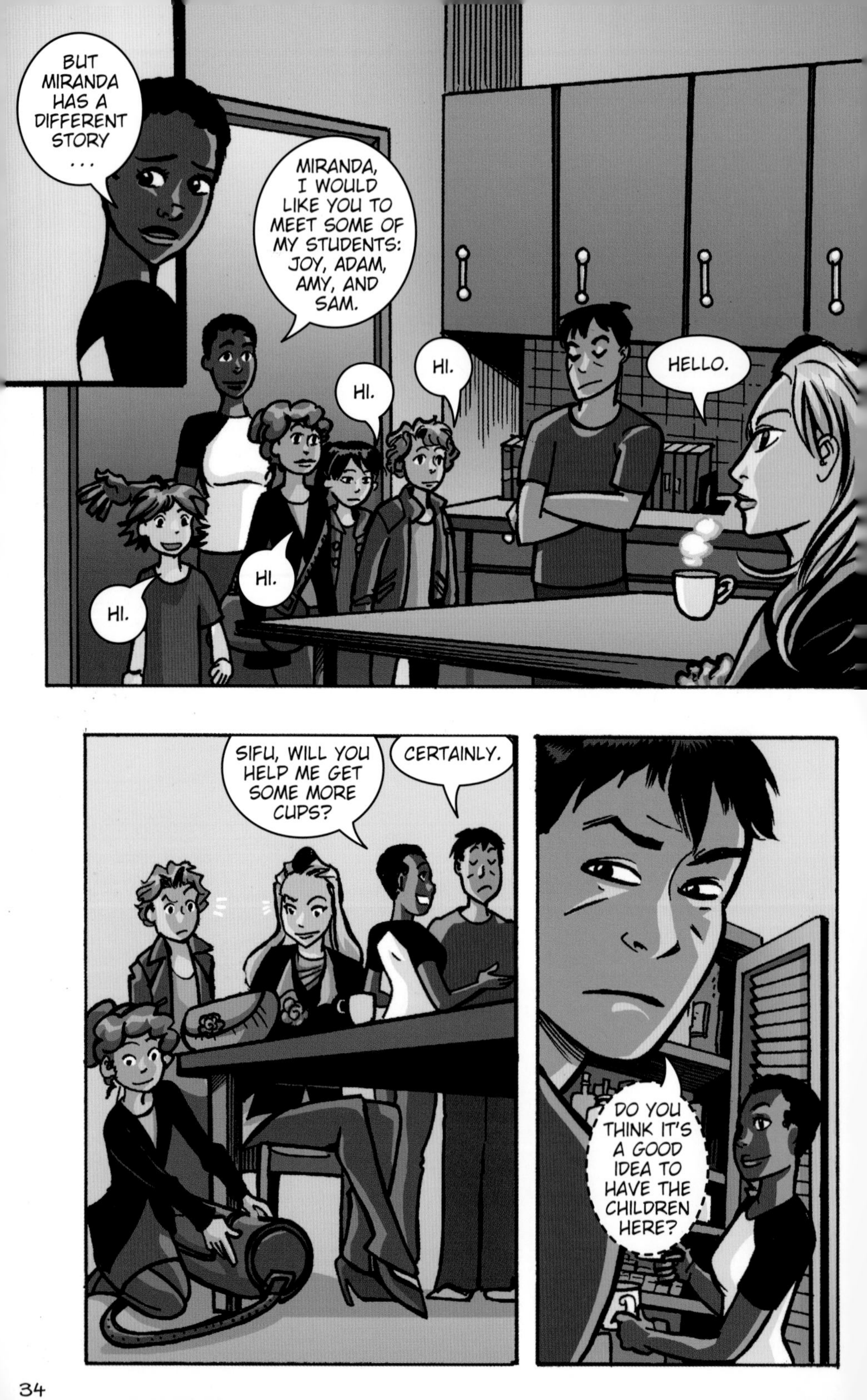
BUT MIRANDA HAS A DIFFERENT STORY . . .
MIRANDA, I WOULD LIKE YOU TO MEET SOME OF MY STUDENTS: JOY, ADAM, AMY, AND SAM.
HI.
HI.
HI.
HI.
HELLO.
SIFU, WILL YOU HELP ME GET SOME MORE CUPS?
CERTAINLY.
DO YOU THINK IT'S A GOOD IDEA TO HAVE THE CHILDREN HERE?

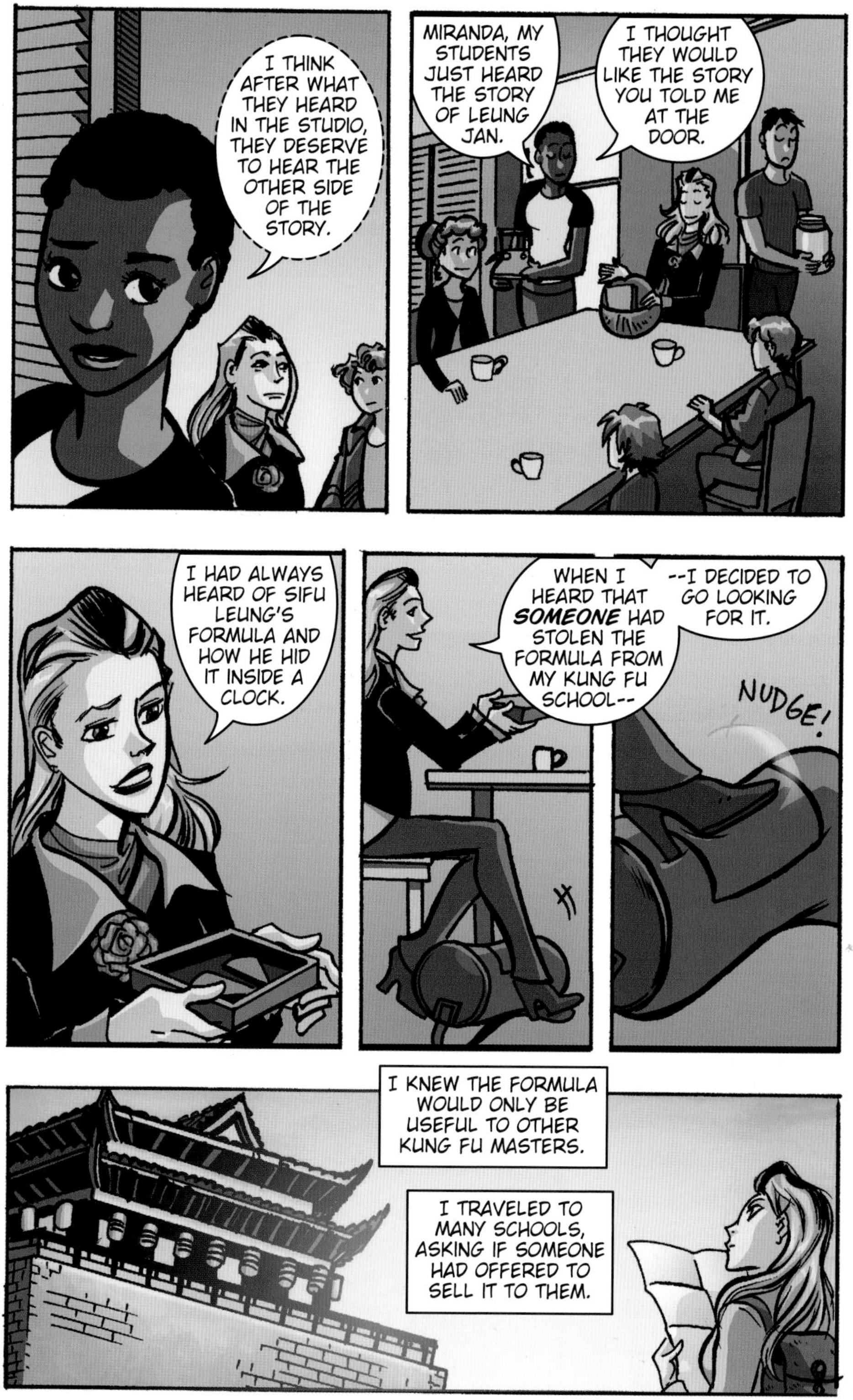
I THINK AFTER WHAT THEY HEARD IN THE STUDIO, THEY DESERVE TO HEAR THE OTHER SIDE OF THE STORY.
MIRANDA, MY STUDENTS JUST HEARD THE STORY OF LEUNG JAN.
I THOUGHT THEY WOULD LIKE THE STORY YOU TOLD ME AT THE DOOR.
I HAD ALWAYS HEARD OF SIFU LEUNG'S FORMULA AND HOW HE HID IT INSIDE A CLOCK.
WHEN I HEARD THAT ***SOMEONE*** HAD STOLEN THE FORMULA FROM MY KUNG FU SCHOOL--
--I DECIDED TO GO LOOKING FOR IT.
NUDGE!
I KNEW THE FORMULA WOULD ONLY BE USEFUL TO OTHER KUNG FU MASTERS.
I TRAVELED TO MANY SCHOOLS, ASKING IF SOMEONE HAD OFFERED TO SELL IT TO THEM.

I MET A KUNG FU MASTER WHO HAD LEARNED FROM ONE OF SIFU LEUNG'S FORMER STUDENTS.

HE ALSO KNEW ABOUT THE FORMULA, BUT HE TOLD A VERY DIFFERENT STORY FROM THE ONE I'D HEARD.

HE CUT THE DISK INTO 8 PIECES.

HE SAID SIFU LEUNG NEVER KEPT THE DISK INSIDE A CLOCK.

$\frac{1}{8}$ $\frac{1}{8}$ $\frac{1}{8}$ $\frac{1}{8}$ $\frac{1}{8}$ $\frac{1}{8}$ $\frac{1}{8}$ $\frac{1}{8}$

1 DISK DIVIDED INTO 8 PIECES. EACH PIECE IS $\frac{1}{8}$ OF A DISK.

EACH DISCIPLE GOT TWO OF THE EIGHT PIECES-- SO EACH HAD $\frac{1}{4}$ OF THE FORMULA.

HE THOUGHT IF EACH ONE ONLY KNEW PART OF THE FORMULA, THE DISCIPLES WOULD HAVE TO STAY FRIENDS--

--BUT IT DIDN'T WORK OUT THAT WAY.

THE SIFU I MET HAD THESE TWO PIECES. HE SAID THEY WERE USELESS WITHOUT THE REST, SO HE SOLD THEM TO ME.

MIRANDA HAS $\frac{2}{8}$, OR $\frac{1}{4}$, OF A DISK!

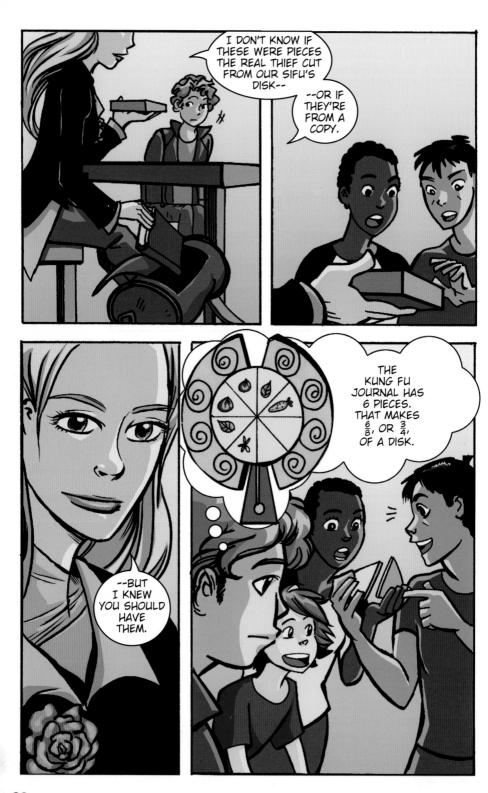

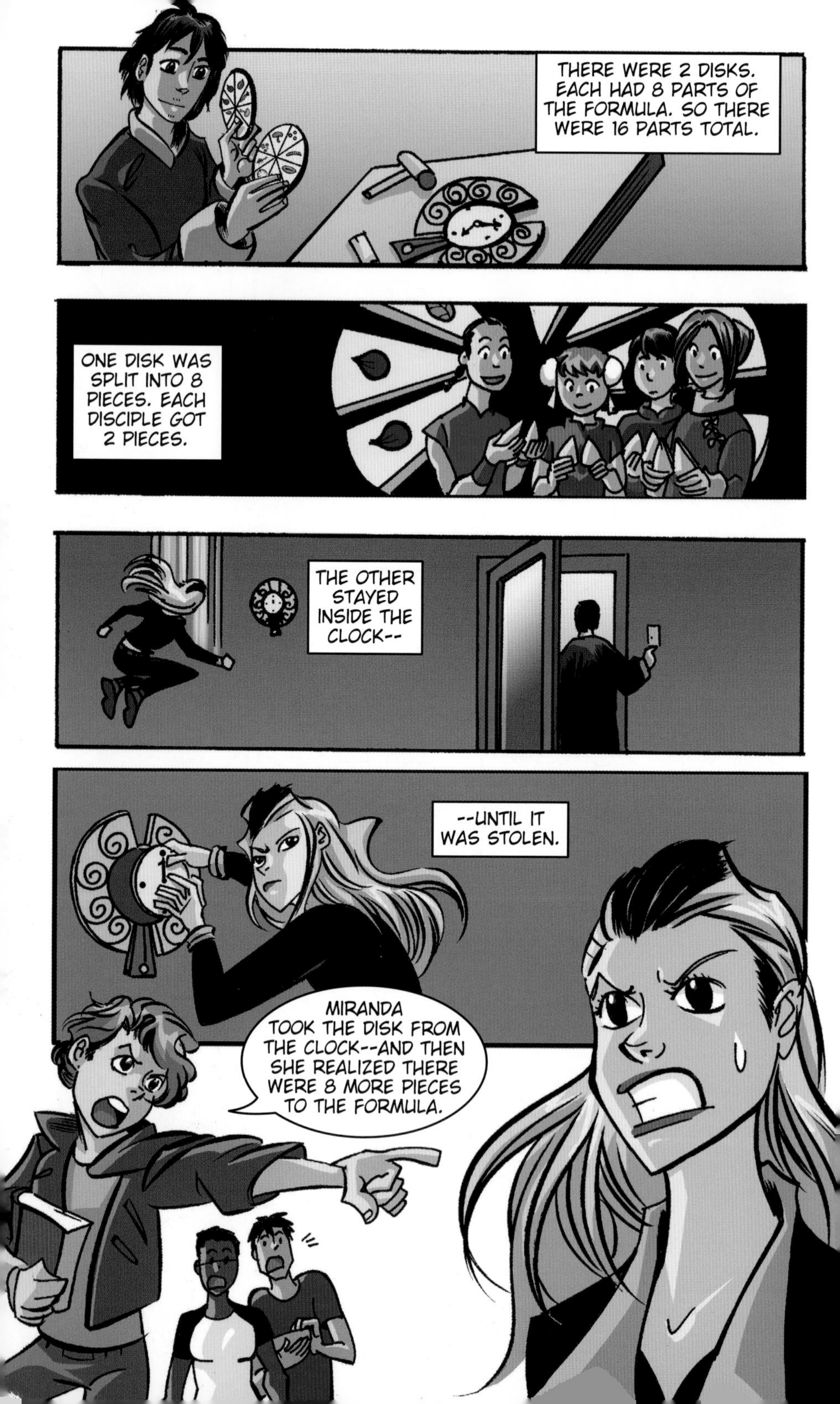
THERE WERE 2 DISKS. EACH HAD 8 PARTS OF THE FORMULA. SO THERE WERE 16 PARTS TOTAL.
ONE DISK WAS SPLIT INTO 8 PIECES. EACH DISCIPLE GOT 2 PIECES.
THE OTHER STAYED INSIDE THE CLOCK--
--UNTIL IT WAS STOLEN.
MIRANDA TOOK THE DISK FROM THE CLOCK--AND THEN SHE REALIZED THERE WERE 8 MORE PIECES TO THE FORMULA.

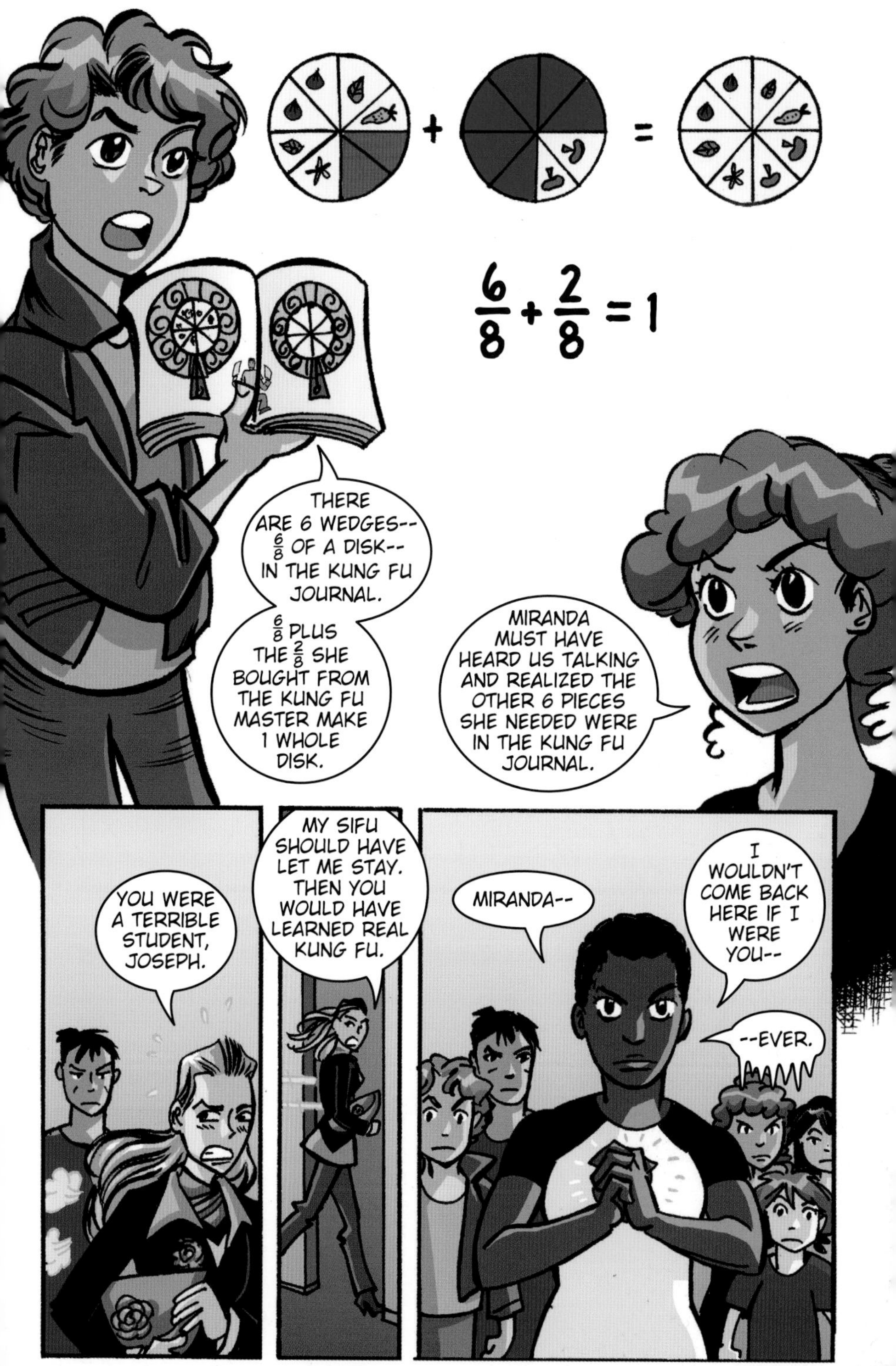
$\frac{6}{8} + \frac{2}{8} = 1$
THERE ARE 6 WEDGES-- $\frac{6}{8}$ OF A DISK-- IN THE KUNG FU JOURNAL.
$\frac{6}{8}$ PLUS THE $\frac{2}{8}$ SHE BOUGHT FROM THE KUNG FU MASTER MAKE 1 WHOLE DISK.
MIRANDA MUST HAVE HEARD US TALKING AND REALIZED THE OTHER 6 PIECES SHE NEEDED WERE IN THE KUNG FU JOURNAL.
YOU WERE A TERRIBLE STUDENT, JOSEPH.
MY SIFU SHOULD HAVE LET ME STAY. THEN YOU WOULD HAVE LEARNED REAL KUNG FU.
MIRANDA--
I WOULDN'T COME BACK HERE IF I WERE YOU--
--EVER.

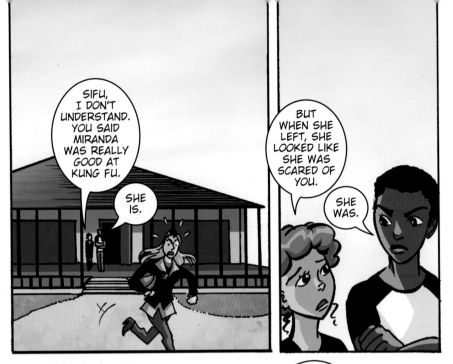

THE NEXT DAY.

DO YOU ALL HAVE YOUR NOTEBOOKS?

YES, SIFU!

AND I'M GLAD YOU THREE COULD JOIN US TOO.

SAM IS RIGHT.

KUNG FU MASTERS ARE TOO SECRETIVE.

LEUNG JAN'S JOW

AND NO ONE WILL BE ABLE TO STEAL LEUNG JAN'S FORMULA.

NOW ALL OF YOU HAVE YOUR OWN KUNG FU JOURNALS.

YOU CAN'T STEAL A SECRET THAT EVERYONE KNOWS.

45